Jane Doe

Lillian Duncan

Jane Doe

Contact Information: titleadmin@pelicanbookgroup.com

All Scripture quotations, unless otherwise indicated, are taken from the Holy Bible, New International Version(R), NIV(R), Copyright 1973, 1978, 1984, 2011 by Biblica, Inc.™ Used by permission of Zondervan. All rights reserved worldwide. www.zondervan.com

Cover Art by *Nicola Martinez*

Harbourlight Books, a division of Pelican Ventures, LLC
www.pelicanbookgroup.com PO Box 1738 *Aztec, NM * 87410

Harbourlight Books sail and mast logo is a trademark of Pelican Ventures, LLC

Publishing History
First Harbourlight Edition, 2020
Paperback Edition ISBN 978-1-5223-0276-6
Electronic Edition ISBN 978-1-5223-0275-9
Published in the United States of America

Dedication

This and all I do is for God's glory.

To Ronny, for all your love and support.

A special shout out to Kathy (Brazee) Thompson,
Triway Class of 1973!

What People are Saying

Trapped

Tense, gripping, challenging. and redemptive.
~Jennifer from CarpeDiem

You certainly want to read this book in the daytime, with the doors locked and your phone close by.
Betti Mace, Betti Mace Book Reviews

Trapped by Lillian Duncan is a phenomenal work of romantic suspense. This is the first book that I have read by this author but I have read many books in this genre and I was interested in the premise of this book. I am in awe of the author's ability to create terrifying situations that seem way too real.
~Michelle Castaneda, Reviewer, Livin' Lit:

Reading the first few pages of this book made me want to run and hide.
~Deana Dick, reviewer, Texas Book-aholic

This is a book that will grab you from the first page, and when you're a few pages in you begin to think that the story is almost over, but no! . . .I will be looking for more books by this author.
~Maureen Timerman, Maureen's Musings

1

"Wakey. Wakey. Little Suzie." His sing-song voice penetrated the drug-induced blur that was her normal these days.

"Not...my... name." Raven. Her name was Raven Lynn Marks. It was getting harder and harder to remember anything about her life before the monster, but she didn't want to forget her name. Raven. Her name was Raven. That was all she had left.

The monster had taken everything else from her.

Her life. Her family. Her friends. She refused to let him take her name. As she ran her fingers through her long, black, stringy hair, the weight of the chain around her wrist chafed. She looked up at him. "Leave...me...alone."

"You'd like that, wouldn't you, Little Suzie? But you don't tell me what to do." A moment later he poked her with the electric cattle prod.

The electrical current traveled throughout her body causing her to jerk and tremble. Her mind tried to block out the excruciating pain. It failed. She screamed.

He chuckled. "That's more like it. You thought you were so strong but look at you now." He waved the wand toward her as if performing a magic trick. Deliberate. Slow. Taunting her.

No doubt he wanted to savor her fear. She wished she were strong enough to hide it since he so enjoyed causing it, but that time had passed long ago. "Just kill me."

The cattle prod stopped moving toward her. His face was hidden as always by the ski mask, but she could still see his eyes and his mouth. His gaze was intent as if she were a bug specimen in science class. "Really? Is that really what you want? To die?"

"Yes, that's really what I want. Please just kill me. I can't do this anymore. I want to die. Isn't that what will happen anyway? Sooner or later. Please make it sooner. Show me a little mercy. Please."

The black ski mask moved as his lips curled into a smile. Cruel, but still a smile. "Wow! What a rush to have that kind of power. I guess that makes me god." He laughed. "At least, your god, Suzie Q." Without warning, he poked her with his cattle prod once again.

More voltage this time.

Her body jerked on its own accord. She couldn't control the tremors. Her eyes rolled back in her head. Slobber drooled from her mouth. Her limbs twitched — and kept twitching. "Please, God, let me die." She wasn't sure if she said the words out loud or merely thought them. When the tremors stopped, Raven stared up at her captor.

He stood there watching her.

She'd never seen the monster's face—only his eyes. Cold. Not true. They weren't cold, but full of hate. What had she done to deserve that kind of hate?

Why was she here? The fact that she hadn't seen his face used to give her hope that he might free her. Someday. But that hope was dwindling fast. She was pretty sure she'd die here. Alone. And in pain. Nobody would ever know what happened to her. Her poor sister. What was she thinking? Was she still looking for her? Or had they forgotten her? Raven knew the answer—her sister would never give up looking for her.

The monster knelt down beside her.

If she could pull off that mask. See the monster's face. That would be a victory. She wanted to see his face. Her hand moved up a few inches, but the fear won. Her hand fell back on the dirty cement floor.

"Why are you here?" No longer her tormentor. Now he was the teacher and she was the student.

They'd been through this before—many times. She knew the answers he wanted—what she was supposed to say, but she still had a little defiance left in her. Summoning her energy, she glared at him. "Because you're a monster."

Cattle prod.

He asked again. His voice calm but it was the calm before the storm. "I asked, why are you here?"

She looked at the cattle prod in his hand. The defiance was gone. She gave the answer he wanted to hear. "Because I'm a self-centered, celebrity-seeking narcissist."

"Much better, Suzie Q."

She glared. "That's not my name."

Cattle prod.

"Your name is whatever I say it is, and I say it's Suzie Q. Today. Tomorrow it might be something else. Because it's whatever I say. Because I am your god. I decide if you live or die. Or even eat."

Cattle prod.

"What's your name?"

She didn't answer.

"I asked you a question." The cattle prod moved closer.

"Suzie."

"Much better." She could see his grin through the hole in the ski mask. "And who am I?"

She summoned her courage and met his gaze. "A monster."

Cattle prod.

"I don't know why you make me do this to you. You do know it's all your fault. I'm a patriot. I'm not a cruel person. I love America and people like you are trying to ruin it. Not just for me but for everyone in this wonderful country. I can't let you do that. Now who am I?"

She didn't understand why he felt the need to justify what he was doing to her. There was no justification in the world for what he was doing to her. All she understood was that she didn't want any more pain, so she gave him the answer he wanted. "A patriot who loves America."

"Much better. Who are you?"

"A self-centered, celebrity-seeking narcissist."

"I'm glad we understand each other. Remember this is not my fault. It's your fault."

Cattle prod. And again and again.

She screamed and begged him to kill her until her world went black.

2

Raven regained consciousness but didn't open her eyes. Instead she listened. Was the monster still here? Was he standing above her? Staring down at her? Waiting for her to wake up so he could induce even more pain. Or had he left?

Sometimes he left for days.

She prayed for those days—even though it meant no food. It also meant no pain. Other days, he might visit two, three or even four times. This had been one of those days. She thought it had been a three-visit day. So far. When she decided she was alone she opened her eyes.

He was gone but nothing else had changed. She still had a thick chain wrapped around her left ankle and another around her right wrist. She was sprawled out on a slightly damp concrete floor. In the corner of her prison, her captor had tossed some straw or hay— she wasn't sure which—he said for her comfort.

Yeah, some comfort. She looked at the two aluminum dog bowls. Dog bowls. That's what her life had been reduced to. Eating and drinking from dog bowls. Had he filled them while she was unconscious? Some days he did and some days he didn't. When he filled them that usually meant he might not be around for a while. She'd learned to eat sparingly or risk hunger for many days.

Summoning her energy, she crawled over to the bowls.

They were empty.

Her eyes filled with tears.

He would be back. Soon.

So hungry. So thirsty. She sat by the empty bowls sobbing. After a time, she used her dirty shirt to wipe her nose, and then looked around her prison.

The room had only one small window that was half-caked in dirt, so she was always in semi-darkness even during the daytime. The floor was cement, and the walls were wooden. Her chains were connected to screws in the floor but had cement covering them. She'd tried to dislodge them many times. She'd finally given up trying. She assumed she was in a barn, not just because of the straw but the smell. The place definitely smelled like a barnyard.

She had no idea how long it had been since she'd breathed fresh air without the stench. The truth was she wasn't exactly sure how she'd even gotten to her prison because of the drugs. She didn't know what kind of drugs he used, but they made her confused. She forgot things. Important things.

But not her name. Raven Lynn Marks. It felt like a victory. No matter how often he called her that stupid name, he couldn't make her forget her real name. And he couldn't make her forget that somewhere, people worried about her, prayed for her, and loved her.

She wondered if anyone loved the monster. She couldn't imagine that was even possible. He seemed to have lost every shred of humanity. But he must have some sort of life outside of her prison.

She just couldn't imagine what it might be.

Raven touched the empty dog bowls. She had no doubt he was drugging her food or water. But that was OK with her. It made the time go by faster when she slept. It wasn't like she had a choice anyway. He fed her so little that she had to eat what he gave her—even if it was drugged.

Sleep was good but remembering was better. She needed to remember things. Important things not just her name. How had she gotten here? She tried to focus. She'd tried to remember day after day but couldn't. It was as if her mind was a chalkboard that had been completely erased. She could remember her life. Her family. Her job. Her little apartment. But she couldn't remember how she got here.

What she did remember was waking up in this prison and not being allowed to leave it. No matter how often she'd begged the monster to let her outside even for a few minutes, he refused.

This room was the only room. He kept that door shut and her chains weren't long enough to reach the door anyway. The door—her way to freedom. It probably wasn't even locked. If she could get the chains off, she might be able to just walk out and go home.

Tears filled her eyes.

Home. Her sister. Her nieces. Marnie and her other friends. What did they think happened to her? Were they still looking for her? Or had they given up? She closed her eyes willing the thoughts to go away. It was too painful to think about her past life. It was gone. This was her life now. She opened her eyes. Her gaze moved around her new life—her prison. Her chains only let her move around in this one area.

Her approximation was that the room was about five feet by eight feet. Her captor's chains gave her enough leeway to walk about half the length and width of the room. But not quite long enough to reach the door.

The door. It seemed magical to her. If only she could get to the door, she might have a chance. Tears streamed down her cheeks. But she didn't have a chance.

The monster had all the power.

Still she did her best to stay in shape by walking and running in place and even calisthenics when she was feeling strong enough. After all, she needed to keep up her strength—just in case she ever got an opportunity to escape.

It hadn't happened yet—but that didn't mean it couldn't—wouldn't happen. She prayed and prayed for it to happen but no answer came from God. Maybe someday. Maybe even today. Unfortunately, if it happened today, she wasn't sure it would make a difference.

The last session had been difficult. Maybe the worst since she'd been here. She couldn't survive many more like that. She knew she should get up—to move, but there was too much pain. And what would be the point?

The truth was she really didn't care anymore. She hadn't been lying when she'd told the monster to kill her. She'd meant every word. She couldn't do this any longer. "Please, God. I'm sorry I'm not strong enough. I don't know how Jesus did it. Don't let him hurt me again. Please. Just let me die."

The dampness of the floor soaked into her clothes. The stench of the barn surrounded her. Her gaze moved to the corner with the straw. Should move there…might be more comfortable…but she didn't have the energy to even try.

The darkness of her dreams came once again.

Sometime later, she heard a noise and then felt a kick in her side. She sucked in her breath with the pain. The monster was back. She opened her eyes. A new day? He stood above staring down at her. "So you're finally up. I guess I know where the Lazy Susan got its name."

"My name…not Suzie."

Another kick.

Pain radiated throughout her body.

"It's whatever I want it to be. And I say it's Suzie Q."

Raven. My name's Raven. She wanted to protest but what would be the point? Instead she closed her eyes and waited.

"Open your eyes."

She did as she was told.

"You really are disgusting, you know that, Suzie?" A slight kick again. "I mean, really? Don't you have any pride in yourself? You're filthy. And this place smells horrible. I think it's time for a good spring cleaning, don't you?"

Was it spring? Did that mean she'd been here for a year? Was that even possible? To live this way for that long. Would she be here next year in the spring? And the next? Please help me, God. Please help me.

He walked out of the room but a moment later came in holding a bucket with a scrub brush in one hand and three-gallon jugs of bleach in the other. "Clean this place up. I'll take out the straw. If you do a good job, I might even let you take a bath. Wouldn't you like that?"

She nodded but didn't move.

After he gathered up the straw, he kicked her again for good measure. "What are you waiting for? I said clean this mess up."

"I need my hands. Both of them." She held up her chained wrist.

"I suppose you do." He knelt down and unlocked the padlock.

The chain slipped away. It felt wonderful not to have that heavy thing on. This was the first time he'd unchained her since she'd been here. Maybe this really would be the day? "How about my leg? I can't reach the other part of the room."

"I suppose you can't but that's not happening, Suzie Q. Clean the areas you can reach and then I'll think about unchaining you. Later."

Raven nodded. She picked up one of the bleach containers and poured some in the corner, then moved the bucket closer. It was half-filled with water. She got down on her hands and knees. Using the scrub brush, she did as she was told. The bleach fumes burned her nose and throat.

Her mind wandered. Would he unchain her to let her finish the other side of the room? If he did, could she find a way to get away from the monster? She would. God was with her. With God, all things were possible.

"I know what you're thinking."

She jumped. She hadn't realized he was so close behind her. "If I were you, I'd stop thinking about escaping and find a way to make me like you better."

Raven kept her back turned from him. He might have total control over her body but not over her thoughts. He couldn't stop her from thinking what she wanted.

He watched probably to make sure she was being thorough. After ten minutes or so he left but didn't close the door.

That had never happened. She could hear him out in another area of the barn—if it was a barn. Edging toward the door as far as the chains would let her go, she peeked out. Horse stalls and then the sound of a whinny. Definitely a barn—a very old one. There was nothing modern about this rickety old building. It must have been standing a long time.

Rays of sunshine danced on the straw-covered cement floor.

Her eyes filled with tears at the beauty of it. How long had it been since she'd actually seen the sun? Or been outside? Or felt the soft breeze? She didn't know. Could it really have been a full year? It didn't feel that way, but all her days and nights blurred together. The only thing that separated them was when the monster showed up and hurt her.

Her gaze landed on a nail. Just inside the door. The monster must have kicked it in without noticing. Or was it a trick? One more thing he could punish her for. Could she reach it? She pulled until the chain around her ankle was taut. She reached out. Another few inches but still couldn't touch the nail. She laid flat on the floor stretching her arm. Her finger touched the nail. Carefully, she rolled it toward herself. And then she had it.

The sound of footsteps made her hurry back to the bucket.

It felt like a victory to get the nail. But why? What could she do with it? She couldn't overpower the monster with a silly little nail. Still she had it, and he didn't know she had it. That was something...unless it was a trick.

As she poured more bleach, she stared at the container. If she drank enough of it would it kill her? She knelt down and scrubbed. She thought it might. But she wasn't sure. What if it just made her sick but didn't kill her? That could be worse than dying. Best not to risk it.

As much as she wanted to end this torment; she didn't want to be the one to make it happen. That was God's job, not hers. And not the monster's. Or it shouldn't be the monster's decision, but she had a feeling she knew why he was forcing her to clean the room.

Her time here was coming to an end.

She closed her eyes. It's OK, God. I'm ready to come home. To be with You. To end this torment and suffering. To be in a place with no pain and no tears. Only peace and joy.

But she hated the thought that this monster would get away with this.

And what if she wasn't his first victim—or his last?

She moved as close to the doorway as she could get. Couldn't see him but she could hear him moving around out there. Maybe doing his own spring cleaning. She hurried back to the bleach and poured a big puddle on the floor and kept scrubbing.

The nail was still in her hand. It felt good. Her gaze moved to the little window. Then she had an idea. She walked over to it. Using the nail, she scratched the letter R. Then she hurried back to the scrub brush. Then took a chance again. This time she scratched the

A and V before she lost her nerve and went back to scrubbing.

Scrub. Scratch. Scrub. Scratch. When she was finished, her name, Raven Lynn Marks, and the year, were written on the tiny wooden windowsill. She stared at it for a long moment. Then she spit on it. Once. Twice. She waited as the wetness disappeared.

Her DNA. But she didn't know enough to know whether it would last, but she smiled. Her name. It was proof she'd been in this horrible place.

She quickly moved back to her knees and continued scrubbing.

He poked his head in several times. Each time he found her on her knees scrubbing just the way he'd told her to. When she was finished with the parts she could reach, she sat in the middle of the room and waited.

He walked in and sniffed. "Oh, that's better. Much better."

"Your wish is my command."

"I'm glad you understand that, Suzie Q." He stared down at her. "What are you smiling about?"

"Just enjoying the smell of clean." Hopefully, someday someone would find her name and know what this monster had done to her.

3

"I promised if you did a good job, I'd let you get cleaned up. And I'm a man of my word. Time for that bath. Stand up."

She stood.

"Put your hands out."

She did as she was told.

He wrapped gray duct tape around them. Not handcuffs, but it might as well have been since it did the same job. Her hands were basically worthless. No way to escape. Not true, she reminded herself. With God, all things were possible.

"Can't have you trying to escape now, can we?"

She refrained from saying anything. Over time, she'd found it best to not antagonize the monster. Though there were times she did it anyway. But this wasn't one of those times.

She was curious to see what he planned for her. A bath? Or was it time to end her suffering? Either way would be a win as far as she was concerned. She was tired of feeling so dirty. She stood there quietly, praying and waiting.

He leaned down. As he was unlocking the chain around her ankle, she wished she had something to hit him with and the courage to do it. But she didn't. He was much stronger than she was and using her bare hands against him would only make him angry.

And that meant more punishment.

She didn't want to be hurt anymore. If it was her time to die—so be it.

He grabbed her arm and led her out of the room then shoved her against the wall. "Don't move."

He walked in and picked up the bucket and the empty bleach jugs. She held her breath. Would he look at the windowsill? Would he see her name? If he did, he'd make it disappear and then no one would ever know what happened to her.

He tossed the water on the spot where she'd been sitting. No doubt cleaning up any forensic evidence that she'd ever been in the room—no evidence of her torture. Or of his evil. He was washing away her very presence. Or so he thought.

She opened her hand, staring at the nail, and then let it fall on the floor. It clunked. She held her breath, hoping he wouldn't hear.

He turned toward her. "What did you do?"

"Nothing."

He walked out of the room and stared hard at her. Then looked down at the nail. "Where did this come from?"

She held her breath. Please God don't let him see my name.

He picked up the nail and turned toward her. "Did you see this?"

She shook her head.

"Good thing. Maybe you would have tried to kill me with it. Nail Death instead of Death Knell." He laughed and laughed. When he stopped, he looked at her. "Didn't you like my joke?"

Lillian Duncan

"I don't have much of a sense of humor these days."

"I can see that. That's too bad. I've been told I have a great sense of humor. It's one of my strengths." After one last inspection, he walked out of her prison room and propped the bucket against the wall. "Let's go, Suzie Q. Time's a wasting. Obviously, I can't take you up to my house for a bath, but I'll keep my word."

"Why not? Is your wife up there? Does she know she's married to a monster?"

He moved close. "I'd be careful what you say to me. I'm in a good mood today. But if you make me angry, you'll regret it."

Could she get the ski mask off? She wanted to see his face before she died. If she saw his face, she might understand why he was doing this to her. She looked down. "Sorry."

"That's better. Anyway, I'm not going to renege on my promise. You will definitely be getting wet today." He held up an open can of soda. "Drink this."

She was sure it was drugged, but so what? He placed the open can in her hands. She lifted it to her mouth and took a long drink. It tasted so good. And the sugar—she could almost feel it making its way through her body—energizing her. By the time she'd finished, she felt the drugs beginning to relax her in spite of the sugar and the caffeine. She looked at him. "Thank you."

He started to say something but grabbed her arm instead. "Let's go get that bath. But I'm warning you—no funny business."

Her legs and feet weren't working right—and her head was spinning. The drugs? So fast? He must have put a lot in the soda. She stumbled and fell to her knees. His hands slipped from her arm. Her gaze fell on the rake in front of her. Should she go for it? Taking a deep breath, she grabbed the rake handle and jumped up at the same time. She turned and swung at him. The blow landed on the side of his head. She swung again.

He managed to grab the handle and moved toward her. Anger radiated from him. Each step brought him closer to her. Using her bound wrists, she tried to hit him. But his hand grabbed hers. It was over. She'd lost. But she wouldn't—couldn't give up. She turned and ran.

Seconds later, he grabbed her hair.

She screamed, hoping—praying someone would hear her.

He dragged her across the barn. "You might as well save your breath, Suzie Q. No one's here but me. Nobody to hear you. Nobody to rescue you."

She screamed louder.

He pulled her hair even harder. Tears sprang up. Then without warning he let go. She tumbled to the floor. "Now, you've made me mad. I warned you to not try anything, but you didn't listen. You're going to wish you'd listened." He grabbed her arm and pulled her up.

Raven reached out to grab the ski mask.

He punched her in the stomach.

She doubled over as she gasped for air. "You're a monster."

His face contorted. "Maybe so, but you're the one who's dying today. Not me. And all because you couldn't mind your own business. My secrets are my business, not yours. You should have stayed out of my business."

"I guess we're not pretending that I'm going for a bath anymore."

"I guess you're right." He took the end of the rake he was still holding and hit her in the stomach with it.

Gasping in pain, she said, "Why are you doing this?"

His answer was to punch her in the stomach once more. While she was bent over, he hit her head.

She fought against the darkness. Her head hurt. Her stomach hurt. Actually, there wasn't any part of her that didn't hurt. But her head—foggy. Couldn't think. She reach up with her bound hands and touched something sticky. Blood. Would she bleed out? Her brain turned fuzzy and the dark descended.

~*~

Where was she? Raven opened her eyes and took a deep breath. Fresh air. She sucked in more. What was happening? She struggled to clear her mind. There'd been sunshine in the barn and the smell of bleach as she'd scrubbed away her very existence. The nail. Scrubbing and scratching. The fog cleared as she remembered the fight.

She turned her head to see the sky. She was in something that was moving. A machine that hummed through the floor she was laying on. Not a car. She angled her head up. It was dark now. Stars twinkled above her. The faint outline the vehicle took a moment for her gaze to decipher. She was riding in a golf cart. How long had she been unconscious? I'm ready, Father. To come home. To be with You.

The golf cart stopped moving. The motor shut off. And then it was quiet. He whistled as if he was happy. He really was a monster. "Oh, you're awake, Suzie Q. How nice for you. I did promise you a bath, and so you will have one."

"Monster."

He scooped her up. "That's not very nice. After all, I'm only doing what you asked. You're the one who asked me to kill you. That makes it your responsibility, not mine. None of this is my fault."

"I changed my mind."

"Too late."

Her eyelids drooped. She forced them back open. She stared into the eyes of her captor—her murderer. He still had on the ski mask. She would die without ever seeing his face. Without ever knowing why she had to die. "Why? Why are you doing this to me?"

He smiled. "Because I can." He walked to the edge of a cliff.

Her head hung over. She could see the moonlight glistening off the water far below. Then she looked up. At the twinkling stars. God was waiting for her.

"It's been fun, Suzie Q. Bon Voyage." A moment later, he tossed her.

Her gazed focused on the twinkling stars above her. God, I'm coming home. She soared through the air as if she were flying. And then she dropped.

4

"Raven." Her mother's voice sounded far, far away.

But it couldn't be her mother. Her mother was dead.

"Raven, open your eyes."

Her dead mother again. Oh…that must mean she was dead too. Because…why was she dead? Something bad happened, but she couldn't remember exactly what. Her head hurt too bad to think. Oh well…it didn't matt—

"Raven. I mean it. I want you to open your eyes right now. I need to talk to you. Please."

Not her mother's voice.

She forced her eyes open.

Her sister stared down at her. Tears streamed down her cheeks. "You're awa—"

Too hard to keep her eyes open. She let them close. Someone held her hand. It felt safe. She squeezed the hand but didn't have the energy to open her eyes. She drifted back into a dreamless world. The hand was gone the next time Raven became aware of herself. It was quiet.

She opened her eyes. Ceiling tiles above. Machines that had her hooked up to IVs. She was in a hospital.

Not dead. That was probably good. But why was she in the hospital? What happened to her? She fell asleep.

The hand was back. Raven squeezed the hand and opened her eyes.

Her sister stared back at her. "Oh, Raven. Don't be scared. I'm right here with you. You're in the hospital. You'll be OK. You're safe now."

Her throat hurt, but she managed to say, "Don't...leave."

"Oh, sweetie, I'm not going anywhere. I'm right here with you."

"What... happened?" Probably a car wreck.

"Don't worry about that right now. You just rest." He sister touched her cheek. "I love you, Raven."

"Love...you...too." The next time she woke up her sister was gone, but a nurse was standing beside her.

"Welcome back, Raven. My name's Misty. I'm one of your nurses. How are you feeling?"

"Confused." Her voice sounded scratchy, and her throat still hurt.

Misty patted her hand. "I'm sure that's very true. Your sister just stepped out for a few moments. She'll be back before you know it. In the meantime, I'll change a few bandages if that's OK with you?"

She nodded. "Where...?"

"The hospital, dear. You're in the hospital and you're safe."

Safe? Why did everyone keep saying that? "What hospital?"

"You're in Cumberland Medical Center, dear."

She hadn't heard of it. "Ohio?"

"No, dear. Maryland. You're in Cumberland, Maryland."

Maryland? "But...but I live...Ohio. How...?"

"Don't worry about that right now. In fact, don't worry about anything. Just concentrate on getting better. You're safe. And we're taking good care of you. There's nothing for you to do but get better."

She'd said it again. Safe? The nurse started changing bandages. Cuts and bruises covered her body—a lot of bruises. Why couldn't she remember getting them? And how did she get to Cumberland, Maryland? "Throat hurts."

"That's because you were intubated, but that came out yesterday. You probably don't remember since you were heavily medicated."

"Must be a euphemism for being drugged," she mumbled. Her throat burned. "Can I have some water?"

"How about some ice chips?"

She'd take what she could get. "OK."

She was sucking on an ice chip when Amanda walked in. "Oh, Raven, you're finally, really awake."

"Sort of. I'm still very tired. And confused. What happened to me? Why am I here?"

"That's nothing to worry about. The doctor said that you probably wouldn't remember anything." Her sister tried to hug her, being careful not to dislodge any of the wires and tubes. She gave up and touched Raven's cheek instead. "I'm so glad you're awake. I've been so worried."

"What happened? Why am I here?"

Her sister shook her head as she wiped at the tears. "We were hoping you could tell us."

"We?"

Her sister moved aside.

A man stood just inside her room near the doorway. He wore a uniform and pointed to the badge on his chest. "I'm Sheriff Matthew Borden." He smiled. "But you can call me Matt."

"Am I under arrest? Did I do something wrong?"

Before he could answer, one of the many machines she was hooked up to began to beep. Seconds later another man ran in. "What's going on? Y'all shouldn't be in here. She's barely awake. Out all of you."

"But I'm here sister—her next of kin."

"And I need to talk to her."

"Out. No one's talking to her right now. That's an order."

Her sister let go of her hand. "I'll be right out there. I'm not going anywhere, Raven, so don't worry about a thing." She took hold of the man's arm. "Come on."

"But—"

"You heard him. Out."

The beeping slowed. Raven looked up at the man still standing beside her bed. "Are you a doctor?"

"Actually, I'm the head nurse for this shift. The name's Desmond Jackson. I'm sorry about all that. The sheriff sneaked past me when I wasn't looking. But don't worry, he means you no harm. He just wants to ask you some questions, but he'll have to wait for the doctor to give him permission to talk to you. I promise you he won't be bothering you again until you're ready to talk to him."

"I'm confused."

"I know you are. That's partly from the drugs we've been giving to keep you pain-free, and partly from the accident."

"So I was in a car accident?"

"Ahh, not exactly."

The heart monitor started beeping.

"Then what exactly?"

He turned to the monitor, made a few adjustments and then turned back to her. "Look, I'm not really supposed to say anything, but I can see not knowing is causing you stress. And that's the last thing you need."

Even as he said the words, she could feel her body relaxing. "You gave me more drugs, didn't you?"

"Just a tad. And only what the doctor ordered."

"So what happened to me?" Her tongue was feeling thick. She needed the answer before the drugs took over.

"We're really not sure, sweetie. You'll have to be the one to tell us. The important thing is you're safe now." There was that word again. She started to protest but he held up a hand. "It's really not that important. What's important is for you to get some rest."

Raven wanted to disagree but...

Her sister was back in the room when she woke up the next time. Raven took a deep breath and smiled. Her sister's sweet scent—a mixture of perfume and peanut butter. With her eyes still closed, she said, "Hi, sis."

"How'd you know I was here? You haven't even opened your eyes yet."

She opened them. Her sister was sitting in a chair next to her bed. "I smelled peanut butter."

"Oh. I was hungry. and the vending machine had those little peanut butter crackers I love. So you know I ate some."

"Is that policeman still waiting for me?"

"No, that nurse should be a bouncer. The sheriff won't be back until the doctor gives him permission. That was my mistake. I shouldn't have let him come in with me, but he's been worried about you, too."

"I'm confused, Amanda. I don't understand any of this. Why am I in a hospital in Maryland and not at home? What happened to me? Why can't I remember anything? That nurse—what was his name—Des—something like that."

"Desmond."

"Desmond wouldn't tell me why I was in Maryland. How did I get here? What happened?"

Her sister smiled, but there were tears in her eyes. "Do you remember anything?"

Raven tried to think but her mind was a blank. "No...I...I can't remember anything."

"I don't know what happened to you either, but you were found unconscious on the banks of the Cacapon River in West Virginia. And eventually you ended up here. At the Cumberland Medical Center in Maryland."

"I was found in a river? In West Virginia? That can't be right."

"But it is."

"What river did you say?" She was having trouble making sense any of this.

"The Cacapon River. Actually where that river comes into the Potomac. And I don't know what happened to you or how you got there. That's why the sheriff wants to talk to you. To ask you what happened. That's all."

Raven stared at the wall. "I don't know. I can't remember. Anything."

"Don't get stressed about it. The doctor said that might happen. Because of the head injury."

"I have a head injury?"

"Among other things."

Raven looked down at herself. Both legs were wrapped in something like bubble wrap. One arm was immobilized as well. She looked at her injuries—she should be in pain, lots of pain. "I see what you mean. Why don't I hurt?"

"The drugs are keeping you comfortable."

"Must be a lot of drugs."

"But they might be why you're not remembering. You'll probably remember more as they lessen your pain meds."

Raven wasn't sure if she wanted to remember. From the looks of her injuries, something bad must have happened to her. Why couldn't she remember? "OK. Tired." She needed to rest…just for a minute.

5

The next time she woke up her sister was sitting in a chair with her head back sleeping. Amanda's mouth was open, and she was snoring. She must be exhausted to be able to sleep in that position. It looked quite uncomfortable.

Raven fought the urge to call out to Amanda. But she looked as if she needed the rest. No one else was in the room. She closed her eyes, trying to remember. It didn't work. When she opened her eyes, her sister was staring at her. "You're awake."

"I've been awake. You were the one snoring."

Amanda wiped at the drool on her mouth. "I don't snore."

"So you say, sis."

A woman in a white jacket marched in. She was on the short side and probably in her fifties. Her short brown hair had a reddish tint. Though she was diminutive, she had an air of authority about her. She slipped on glasses as she picked up a chart. After reading it, she turned her attention to Raven and smiled. "I'm Dr. Schaeffer. Melly Schaeffer. My patients usually call me Dr. Melly. It's good to see you awake, finally."

"Finally? How long have I been here?"

"I'll answer your questions as best I can, but you have to remain calm. If you get too upset, I'll have to up your medications, and I'll need to leave along with your sister. Without answering your questions." Dr. Melly's gaze was sharp.

"What day is it?"

"First, I need your promise."

Raven stared at the doctor. What would she say that would be so upsetting she needed a promise to be calm? Had she killed the driver in the other car? That would explain why the sheriff had been here. The machine beeped as her heart rate increased. She took a deep breath. And another. The beeping slowed and then stopped. "I promise."

"Good. Now before I answer you, I have a few questions of my own. I'd like you to take a guess on the date."

Raven wasn't in the mood for games. But the doctor didn't seem to be joking. "OK, well…I'll say I've been here around a week so that would make this about May twelfth."

Amanda gasped. Her hand flew to her mouth as if to stop herself from speaking. Her gaze flew to the doctor.

The doctor stayed focused on Raven. She gave a small encouraging nod. "OK. So that's interesting."

"Well, how close was I?"

"I have a few more questions before I tell you."

"You promised to tell me."

"And I will, Raven. Is that what you want me to call you? Raven?"

"That's my name." Raven was her name but…something else about a name. Something important. Brushing the thought away, she focused on the doctor. She'd think about that later. "I just want to know what day it is."

"I understand that. I'm really sorry to be acting all mysterious. I don't mean to do that, but I need to know a few things. Can you tell me the last thing you do remember? Before waking up in the hospital?"

She'd been trying to do that while Amanda slept. She closed her eyes. What was the last thing she'd been doing? Nothing. A blank screen. "I…I can't remember."

"OK. No problem. Can you tell me where you live?"

"I…I live in Marietta. Ohio." She looked over at Amanda. "Right?"

"Right." Her sister looked as if she might pass out. What was going on here?

"And what kind of a job do you have, Raven?"

"I'm a writer. For the Marietta News. An investigative reporter, mostly. I do some freelancing as well."

"Very good. And what's the last memory you have about work?"

"Oh, now I remember. I just finished a three-part series on the presidential race. It got picked up by several papers." Something nudged her brain. Had she been working on something else? Apparently not or she'd remember. "I was going to celebrate with Marnie. She's my boss."

"And did you? Go with your boss?"

"I…I…don't know. Can't remember." She closed her eyes. "Wait a minute, I remember getting dressed and…" She stopped. "And that's all I can remember."

"That's very good, Raven."

"So what day is it?"

"Remember you promised not to get upset."

Her stomach churned as she nodded. Whatever the doctor said would change her life. She took a deep breath. "I'll do my best."

Her sister grabbed her hand and squeezed.

"It's September second."

Her mind stopped working. "I…what…that can't be right. Are you sure? That would mean I've been unconscious for months."

The doctor nodded. "No, you've only been in the hospital for four days."

"Four days? Then how can it be September? You're not making sense." The monitor was beeping.

"I need you to stay calm."

"But what happened? I don't understand."

Beeping.

Amanda squeezed her hand, but tears slid down her cheeks.

More beeping. And then she started to cry, too. How could this be?

"I'm sorry you're upset. We'll talk more later." The doctor turned to the machine.

A moment later, Raven's eyelids fluttered closed.

6

"I filed a missing-persons report on you on May fifth."

"I was missing?"

The doctor was gone when Raven woke up. But Amanda was there, as always. Raven was doing her best to stay calm. None of it made any sense to her. But if the beeping started, they'd give her more medicine, and she'd never get any answers to her questions.

"Yes. You never showed up at the restaurant that night. On May third. You texted Marnie that you would be late for dinner. She was concerned when you didn't show up. She just figured something came up. Probably a story you were working on, but when you didn't show up at work the next day, she called me. We spent the day calling you and your friends. Nobody knew where you were. You just disappeared into thin air. The next day I drove down and filed the report with the Marietta Police."

"Where have I been all that time?"

"We have no idea." Amanda's hands raised in an I-don't-know gesture. "The police eventually found your car at the West Virginia Welcome Center. Do you remember driving there?"

Raven closed her eyes, picturing the welcome

center across the river. She knew it well. "Last time I went there was when we went to Parkersburg to shop for the kids at Christmas time, remember?"

"I remember. It was a good day." Amanda's voice was soft. "Can you think of a reason why you needed to go to West Virginia?"

Raven closed her eyes and then popped them back open. "Nothing. I can't remember even being there that night. I remember getting dressed to go meet Marnie and….that's it. My mind just goes blank."

Dr. Schaeffer walked back in. She looked at Amanda. "How's the patient?"

"Much better. She's being very calm."

"I upped the dosage a bit. To help."

"Doctor, why can't I remember anything?"

"It's probably a combination of things."

"Like what?"

"Your injuries, the pain medication, and…" The doctor sighed. "And to be honest, your mind might not want to remember."

"But I do want to remember."

"A part of you does, but the other part might want to protect you from the truth of what happened to you. At this point, remembering is not a priority. Your physical condition is my concern." She smiled at Raven. "I'm sure all you've heard is distressing. I know it would be for me. But I need you to relax and let the healing begin. We can worry about those details later."

Raven pointed at her battered body. "Is that even possible? For me to heal? Look at me."

"With God, all things are possible, Raven."

"You're a believer."

"I most certainly am. God is the true healer, not me. I may not know what happened to you, but I can tell you that it wasn't your time to go home."

Raven stared. Something about the doctor's words triggered a memory—almost. Then it was gone. She shook her head in frustration. "I need to remember. I have to remember. It's important. Why can't I remember anything?"

"It could be the head injury you sustained in the fall. Your tox screen showed that you had drugs in your system as well. Something popularly known as a date rape drug. It messes with your memory as well as incapacitates you. One of the reasons rapists use it. And there were other drugs as well."

Date rape drug? Had she been raped? She didn't want to think about that. "You think I was in a fall?"

She nodded. "You were found in the Cacapon River near the Potomac. It's a beautiful area actually. Lots of mountains and cliffs. Your injuries are consistent with a fall from a high altitude."

"Do you mean I was thrown off a mountain? And I'm still alive?"

Dr. Melly smiled. "As I said it wasn't your time to go home."

7

"Today's the big day, huh?" Sheriff Matthew Borden walked. He'd visited several times and was always smiling in spite of his frustration with the ongoing investigation about her abduction.

Since Raven couldn't remember anything, the police had virtually no leads to discover what happened to her or who was responsible for it. Most likely, she would never know what happened to her in the months she'd disappeared. Unless she started remembering.

Dr. Melly said that was a definite possibility, but Raven wasn't so sure. When she tried to remember, her mind was blank. "I suppose that's one way to look at it, Sheriff." Raven was in a wheelchair waiting to be transferred to a rehab center. She'd been in the hospital for almost a month but still couldn't walk and her pain was overwhelming at times.

Dr. Melly assured her it would get better, eventually.

Raven wasn't so sure. There were times she wished she'd die in the fall.

"I just stopped in to say good-bye and to let you know that I'll still be working on your case." The sheriff smiled again. "Just because you're out of sight doesn't mean you'll be out of mind. Somebody hurt you, and they need to be held accountable for that. And I plan to make sure they do."

That wouldn't change the fact that her life was ruined. She forced a smile. "I appreciate that."

"If you remember anything, no matter how small or insignificant, you give me a call. Any little thing could make the difference."

"I will, but you didn't have to drive all this way to tell me that." He was a sheriff of Morgan County, West Virginia, where she'd been found. Cumberland, Maryland was out of his jurisdiction.

"I really came to say good-bye and to tell you that you've got a lot of people praying for you and your recovery." He patted her shoulder. "It's bad right now, but it will get better."

Would that ever happen? She couldn't imagine, but with God all things were possible. "Thank you, Sheriff. I'm really sorry I can't remember anything to help with the investigation."

"There's nothing to be sorry about. I'm just glad you'll be all right." He paused. "Eventually. I know it's rough right now and will be for a while, but I have a good feeling about you. You got this."

"I don't know about that."

"I do." Dr. Schaeffer walked in. "I'm with Sheriff Borden. You're stronger than you think, Raven. Most people wouldn't have survived that fall. You did. And God has a reason for that."

"I can't imagine what that could be."

"Maybe not now but eventually you'll find God's purpose. Remember to keep your eyes on God, not your circumstances. He promises to never forsake us. Believe in that promise, Raven, and you'll be OK."

How could she believe that when she felt so alone—so forsaken? If God loved her, why did she have to suffer so much? As soon as she had the thought, another thought came. God's own Son had to suffer—even more than she. She nodded as if to tell God she understood. "I'll try."

"And I expect you to let me know how you're doing. It doesn't have to be every day or even every week but email me every now and then to update me on your progress. OK?" Dr. Melly's stern gaze told Raven she meant it.

"If I ever have any progress, I'll be sure to let you know."

"You will heal. I promise, Raven."

Raven didn't want to argue the point. "I can't thank you enough for everything you've done. And I'll email you soon. I promise."

"It's been a pleasure working with you. You've been a wonderful patient."

"That's because I had a wonderful doctor."

Dr. Schaeffer's cheeks reddened, and then she allowed a small smile. "So, Sheriff, I'm assuming still no leads."

"You assume right."

The doctor looked back at Raven. "Just because you can't remember now doesn't mean you won't at some point in the future. I've been doing some research on memory loss, and it seems that memories are never really lost. So you might still remember even months from now. Anything could trigger a memory. A song, a picture. Even a smell."

"I hope that's true. I hate the thought of whoever did this to me getting away with it."

Sheriff Borden patted her shoulder. "Me, too."

Amanda walked in followed by a man in a white uniform. "Time to go, Raven, if you've said your good-byes." She pointed at Raven. "That's the patient."

Raven laughed. "I think he probably figured that out, Amanda."

Her sister laughed too. "I guess that's true. Ready to go home, Raven?"

Except she wasn't going home or returning to her life. Her old life was over—at least for the foreseeable future. She would be living at the Holmes County Nursing and Rehab center near Millersburg, Ohio, where Amanda and her family lived, to make it easier on her sister.

Raven had no idea when she'd be healthy enough to resume her old life—if ever. At this point, she'd be happy with being able to walk to the bathroom on her own again.

One plane trip, two ambulance rides, and six hours later, Raven sat in the room that would be her home for the foreseeable future—barely more than a hospital room. She tried to be happy, but all she felt was despair. Would this nightmare ever end? With two broken legs and numerous other injuries, Raven couldn't see an end. Or a beginning. No end to her pain. And no beginning to resume her life. As much as she hated it, she was at the mercy of others.

The physical therapist had already made a visit and told her they would start therapy the next day. She'd been all sweet and bubbly—Raven was barely able to be civil to the woman. But the woman hadn't seemed to notice.

The room was private, a fact for which Raven was grateful. She had no desire to talk to anyone about anything. She was tired of putting up the brave front for everyone. She wanted to be left alone. Tears leaked out.

This place had been Amanda's choice. She'd wanted Raven to be close enough to her that she could spend time with her. Raven didn't argue about it since it didn't really matter to her. One place was as good as another.

The only thing that mattered to her at the moment was remembering. If she could remember what happened to her, maybe she could move on—forget about it. How bizarre. She wanted to remember just so she could forget. Life was strange.

8

Raven pressed the button and moved her bed to a sitting position. She hated everything about this place—everything about herself. She wished she'd died when the monster threw her off a cliff. At least if she'd died, she'd be in heaven. Instead of here in pain—and completely helpless.

Amanda walked in. "Hi, Sis. How are you feeling today?"

"You don't want to know."

"I do want to know."

"I doubt that very much."

Amanda was her cheerleader. Optimistic. Always trying to encourage her. Her sister just wanted to help—but Raven was tired. Tired of pretending.

"What's wrong?"

"Really? You ask me what's wrong? Look at me. I can't walk. I can't even go to the bathroom by myself."

Amanda's face turned splotchy red and she bit on her lip. "I know, but—"

"I hate this place."

"It's the best rehab center in the county, but we can find a different place if you want."

"Stop calling it a rehab center. It's a nursing home. A nursing home for old people waiting to die and broken people like me. People who can't take care of themselves."

"It's only temporary, Raven. You're getting better. It's just taking some time."

"Yeah, right." She held up a hand. "Amanda, just go home. Please."

"Why? What did I do wrong?"

"Nothing. You didn't do anything wrong but there's no reason to waste your time coming here, trying to cheer me up. It is what it is, and I'm tired of pretending that everything's OK."

Amanda wiped at tears. "I'm not here to cheer you up. I'm here to see you. I thought I would never see you again during all those months when you were gone. I just want to spend time with you. You can be as cranky as you want. I don't care."

"I don't want to spend time with you. Go home. Take care of your family. They need you. I don't need you. Please just leave."

"You are my family."

Raven rubbed her head. She needed to make Amanda understand. "I'm not trying to be mean, Amanda. Really, I'm not. I just think your time is better spent taking care of your husband and kids. There's nothing you can do for me."

"I'm taking care of them, but I'm not giving up on you, Raven. I know it's hard right now, but it's going to get better. I know it will."

Everyone kept promising her it would get better, but she didn't think so. She was tired and she hurt and she wanted to be left alone. Not pushed and badgered.

Nobody understood. Her life was over. The worst part was she didn't even know why. No matter how hard she tried to remember what happened during those months she was missing, her mind remained a blank.

She wasn't acting the way God wanted her to. She took a deep breath and looked at her sister. Forcing her voice to be calm, she said, "Amanda, I love you, but you coming here every day makes me feel guilty. It makes me feel as if I'm taking you away from your family."

Her sister looked up at the ceiling for a moment then met her gaze straight on. "That's a lie, Raven. That's not it at all. At least be honest with yourself."

Raven hadn't meant for this to turn into an all-out argument. "I'm tired. Please go."

"Tired? I don't know why. From what I hear you refused to go to physical therapy today. And yesterday."

"It's none of your business. Go home and don't come back."

"It's just like when we were kids. You whined and complained because you didn't get to be a cheerleader like me, or be on any sports team, but it was your own fault. You refused to step up and practice. To do what you had to do."

"I had better things to do."

"Yeah, like read a book."

"There's nothing wrong with reading."

"I didn't say there was. But you wanted to be a cheerleader, you were just afraid to try. If you didn't try, you wouldn't fail. And so you never tried."

"So what if I wasn't that physical of a person. So what if I preferred reading to sweating. All the reading helped make me a good reporter."

"I know that, but right now you have to step it up and do what the physical therapist needs you to do. Or you won't get better. You won't be able to walk. Ever. This is too important, Raven. You have to try."

"It's none of your business."

"And speaking of reporting, Marnie tells me you're refusing to talk to her. She tried to give you a couple of different writing assignments and you refused them. You loved being a reporter."

"Not anymore. Reporters are just liars. Their lies are ruining this country. And they're celebrity-seeking narcissists." The words popped out. Where had that come from? She'd never had a thought like that in her life.

Her sister's mouth fell open. "What are you talking about?"

"Never mind. Stay or go, but I'm taking a nap." She turned away from Amanda so her sister wouldn't see the tears. Raven closed her eyes, praying for sleep. It was the only time she had any relief from…the pain. She wasn't sure which was worse—the physical pain or the mental.

Amanda stood by her bedside for a long time, crying.

Raven wiped at her own tears but wouldn't turn back to her sister.

Finally, Amanda left.

Raven's tears turned into sobs. This is just too hard, God. I can't do this.

~*~

"Hello, Raven."

Raven stopped staring at the ceiling and looked

toward the door.

A woman who appeared to be about Raven's own age blocked the doorway with her wheelchair. "Mind if I come in?"

Raven wiped away tears. Time to put on the smiley face, but she wasn't sure if she could. It was getting harder to pretend. "Does it make a difference what I want?"

"Of course it does. I can go if that's what you want."

Raven sighed. "It's fine. Come in. I didn't mean to be rude." But it hadn't stopped her from being rude to Amanda. Her sister had been so good to her and didn't deserve to be treated that way. What was wrong with her? She loved her sister, and yet she'd been so mean to her.

The woman smiled. Her brown hair was short but spikey all over. So cute that it made Raven self-conscious about her own long and scraggly hair. She needed to do something about it.

"I'm sorry I haven't been in to welcome you. I usually give people a few days to get acclimated. It's hard getting used to a new place, so I wait a few days for people to adjust."

Adjust to what? Not having a life? "I don't mean to be rude but I'm really not in the mood for a pep talk or a visit."

"Is that why you think I'm here? To give you a pep talk?"

"Isn't it?" She'd refused to go to physical therapy. And then her fight with Amanda. Nobody seemed to understand that there was no point in any of it. She just wanted people to leave her alone.

"No, I wouldn't call it a pep talk." She touched her

wheelchair. "This chair makes me a realist, not a cheerleader. But your sister did ask me to see you. She's worried about you."

"And exactly who are you?"

"I'm Gracie. I do a little of this and a little of that. Mostly, I'm a counselor and part-time chaplain."

"That means you're supposed to be on my side, right?"

"Right."

"Good. Then tell everyone to leave me alone. If I don't want physical therapy that's my business, right? If I don't want to have my sister visit, that's my business, too."

"Wrong."

"I don't want to be rude, but if you aren't on my side, then I don't want to talk to you."

"Oh, I'm on your side. Make no mistake about that, Raven. But being on your side doesn't mean I'll allow you to hurt yourself and not speak up about it."

"Don't worry about me hurting myself. Someone else already did."

"I know that, and I'm very sorry that happened. But you're the one hurting yourself now. Can't blame that on anyone else. Only you."

"That's my business."

"That's true enough, but I can tell you I'd give anything to not have to use this chair. Even if it meant doing physical therapy eight hours a day. Every day."

Raven stared at the wheelchair, suddenly ashamed of herself. She was being self-centered and narcissistic. It was hard to remember that other people had problems when she had so many of her own. "What happened? An accident?"

"Nope. I'd like to share my story with you, but

only if you want to hear it. It's up to you, Raven."

"It still sort of sounds like it might be a pep talk."

"By the way, Raven's an awesome name. I wish I had a cool name like that."

"Gracie's a good name too."

"Yeah, it's not bad, but it doesn't have the cool factor your does."

"I love your hair. I need to do something with mine."

"I'll have my hair person come in. Would you like that?"

"I guess."

Gracie wheeled herself closer to the bed. "So do you want to hear a little of my story?"

"Sure. As long as you don't tell me everything will be fine. I'm so sick of hearing that."

"I don't blame you. I felt the same way when I had to get in this thing." She patted her chair. "But I've come to love it—sort of."

"You love being in a wheelchair? Why?"

"Because it lets me go places and do things I couldn't do without it. It's not ideal, but it's better than being stuck in my apartment all the time."

Raven stared at Gracie, curious about her story. "Where do you live?"

"I have a small apartment in the assisted living area here. It's in another building but nearby. Makes for an easy commute."

"That's nice. What's your job again?"

"My title is Patient Advocate, but I'm really a counselor and a part-time chaplain. It's not easy adjusting to being here, so I try to help in any way I can. We have a group Bible study once a week. Maybe you'd like to come this week."

"Probably not."

"That's your choice. Anyway… Whatever a patient needs, I try to help them with it."

"Including pep talks, right?"

"I suppose that's one way to describe it, but I like to think of myself as a spiritual advisor. But yes, pep talks are good. We all need encouragement. Especially when life gets tough."

Raven really didn't want a pep talk, but she liked Gracie. "So…tell me your story."

"When I was twenty-five, I was diagnosed with bilateral brain tumors because of a genetic condition called Neurofibromatosis Type 2. NF2 for short."

"Never heard of it."

"Me, either. Even though it's genetic, I'm the first one on my family to have it. But I've learned a lot about it since then. Without going into all the ugly details, the tumors made me deaf and messed up my balance."

"You're deaf?"

Gracie touched her head.

Raven looked at a round object on her head she hadn't noticed before.

"I am, but I received an ABI. An auditory brain implant. It sort of works like a cochlear implant, but it bypasses the auditory nerves that were destroyed by the tumors and goes directly to the brain."

"I would never have guessed."

"Anyway because of the NF2, I can get tumors anywhere and everywhere nerves are in my body. And that's what really put me in the chair. I have several tumors on my spinal cord."

"How awful."

"I can still walk, but it's painful so I don't unless

it's necessary. I won't lie, it's not easy, but it could be so much worse. I mean that literally. There are many people with NF2 that are so much worse off than me. Whenever I start feeling sorry for myself, I remind myself of that."

"I know I should feel that way too but..." She shrugged.

"Don't beat yourself up about it. That doesn't help anything. And besides you're just at the beginning of your recovery. Give yourself time to heal—physically and spiritually. Your sister told me you're a Christian, right?"

Raven nodded.

"More than anything, I've learned that God is faithful. He's there waiting for you so He can do all sorts of good things for you."

"Why doesn't He just do them, then?"

Gracie shrugged. "Sometimes, He does. That's called a miracle, but most of the time we need to keep the faith. His faithfulness and our faith bring on the miracles."

Miracles? That's exactly what she needed. Raven bit her lip. "I think I've lost mine." Her eyes filled with tears at the admission.

"It's OK. God still loves you. Just keep praying and spending time with God. Let Him take care of you now. He is faithful."

Raven wiped at the tears. "I feel so ashamed to admit that I'm not strong. I know I should be but I'm just not. I've been trying to act the right way, but I can't pretend any longer. I just can't do it any longer."

"God doesn't need you to pretend. He just needs you to believe. To have faith. To trust Him."

"I don't know how to do that. It makes me wonder

if I'm even a Christian." More tears rolled down her cheeks at her admission.

Gracie took hold of her hand. "Since I was diagnosed, I've learned to trust God and to stay in the moment. To not worry about the future or to regret the past. To not let my circumstances dictate who I am. I could choose to be angry and bitter about the hand I've been dealt. And for a time I was, but I can tell you trusting God and depending on Him for my peace and joy is much better."

"That sounds like a pep talk, Gracie." Raven smiled through her tears.

"I suppose, but I like to think of it as a God talk not a pep talk. He hasn't forsaken you, Raven. He's there waiting for you, but you need to do your part."

"I thought I was a Christian until this happened. And now, I'm just..." She shrugged. "I don't know what I am anymore."

"You can let your circumstances control you, or you can let them reveal who you are. One thing I've learned, thanks to a lady preacher on TV, is that I can be powerful or I can be pitiful, but I can't be both."

Raven looked at Gracie. "Interesting. I sort of see what you mean."

"Whenever I start feeling sorry for myself, I just start repeating. Powerful or pitiful. Over and over. It's helped me. Maybe it will help you."

"I'll give it a try."

"Nobody told me what happened to you, but I'm assuming you had an accident of some sort."

She'd not planned on telling people about her missing time. It somehow felt shameful to her—as if she'd done something wrong. But Gracie seemed a safe person to talk to. "I don't know what happened to me either. I can't remember anything. I was found in a river in West Virginia many miles from my home in Marietta. I was missing for almost four months."

"Wow. That's awful." Gracie nodded. "No wonder you're angry and confused."

Raven wiped at a tear. "It's so hard."

"I bet."

After they talked for a while, Gracie looked at her watch. "I have another appointment. So would you like to do come to our weekly Bible study?" She held up her hands as if surrendering. "I promise no pep talks, just God talks."

"I guess it couldn't hurt."

Gracie handed her an index card. "Here's a Bible verse that's been helpful to me."

Romans 8: 28

She knew the verse. She looked at Gracie. "Do you really believe this?"

"I *know* it. I hate NF2 and the tumors in my body, but God has worked it out for my good. I have a good life now, and I get to help people. I'm not special. What He did for me, He'll do for you. But…"

"But what?"

"But He can't do it without your cooperation."

"What do you mean?"

"I mean we all have choices in this life. Our choices will either honor God or not honor God."

"And I suppose my choice to not go to therapy doesn't honor God?"

Gracie smiled. "What do you think?"

"I think I have a lot to learn about God."

"Great. Then how about I stop by tomorrow? To see how you're doing. And maybe I'll have another verse for you."

"I'll be here. It's not like I'm going anywhere."

"Yet. But you will one of these days. And remember you can be powerful or pitiful but…"

"I can't be both."

"Exactly, Raven. I know you don't feel as if you have any power right now, but you really do. God lets you choose. You have to make the choice to overcome your circumstances. Or not." Gracie turned her chair and left the room. Amazing Gracie.

Raven wanted what she had— energy and hope in spite of her circumstances. What had Gracie said about circumstances?

You can let your circumstances control you or you can let them reveal who you are. Powerful or pitiful but not both.

Maybe it was time to stop feeling sorry for herself and find God's power that Gracie talked about. God, I choose powerful.

A sense of peace bubbled up and through Raven like a natural spring spilling water over rocks. She sat there, not moving, just enjoying the feeling. And then she knew what she needed to do.

She picked up the phone and dialed Amanda.

9

"Amanda, I don't want to talk to her." Raven whispered.

"Why not? She's your best friend. And why are you whispering?"

"In case she's standing outside my door. Listening. I don't want her to hear me. I don't want to be mean but..." She didn't know how to finish the sentence — couldn't explain her feelings.

"She's out there waiting. I can't just tell her to go away. She drove all the way here from Marietta."

"Yes, you can. Just tell her I don't feel well today and that I'll call her later."

"I'm not lying for you. Do it yourself."

"But...I don't trust her."

Her sister stared at her. "What are you talking about? Of course you trust her. You told me more than once that you'd trust her with your life and your stories."

She couldn't meet Amanda's gaze. "That was before. Before all this."

"Surely, you aren't saying she had anything to do with you being missing. Are you?"

"No. Of course not but she's a reporter. They'll do anything for a story. They can't be trusted."

"That is ridiculous. You're a reporter, and one of the most trustworthy people I know."

She shook her head adamantly. "Not anymore. I'm done with all of that. I refuse to help print lies. Lies that hurt people and this country."

Amanda rolled her eyes. "You really aren't making sense, but I don't have time to argue about this."

"I'm looking for Raven Marks."

Raven recognized the voice in the hall.

Amanda smiled. "Enjoy your visit, sis." She walked out with another word.

Raven steeled herself for Marnie.

But she didn't come in. Amanda must be talking to her. Hopefully, she'd tell her that Raven wasn't up to a visit today. And…apparently not. Raven squelched the spark of anger at her sister.

Marnie was lugging a huge gift basket. "I brought you some gifts."

"I see that. As always, you went overboard."

"Just a little, but it's what I do. Some are from me, but some are from the other re…your other friends. Everybody misses you so much and sends their love."

"That's nice." Raven couldn't look directly at Marnie. She really didn't understand it—couldn't explain why she was having such an adverse reaction to her friend. That was it—focus on Marnie being her friend, not a reporter. Just a friend. Not a reporter. Her muscles relaxed.

Marnie sat down in the easy chair beside her bed. "Oh, my goodness. I didn't expect you to look…" Her words trailed off.

"So bad?"

"So good. You look terrific."

"Nice save, Marnie."

"I love the haircut. It's so cute."

"Thanks. It was such a mess after…you know." Gracie had kept her promise to send in her hair stylist. Raven now had one of those short cuts that puffed in the back and tapered off in the front.

Marnie looked uncomfortable for a moment but forced a smile. "I'm sorry I didn't visit you sooner. I really should have. I could make up an excuse, but I don't really have one."

"That's OK. It's a long drive, and I wasn't up to company anyway." Still wasn't, but she kept that thought to herself. Raven was trying hard to reflect a Jesus-like attitude, thanks to her Bible study/therapy sessions with Gracie.

Marnie's eyes filled with tears, and she grabbed Raven's hand. "I am so sorry. About all of this. What you went through. What you're going through. I can't even imagine."

Marnie—her friend. Raven wiped at her own tears. "It's hard but I'm doing the best I can. When I feel like I can't take my next breath, I call out to God. He's always there."

"You still believe in God after all of this?"

"Especially after this."

"I wish I had that kind of faith."

"I really don't, but I just take it one day at a time. Sometimes one minute at a time."

"I'm impressed."

"Don't be. It's not about me, it's about God."

"I guess. Listen to your doctors and therapists and you'll be running a marathon soon."

Raven tapped her leg. "I don't know about all that. The therapy doesn't seem to be helping at all. I can't even stand up by myself."

"You sound a little depressed, but considering everything, it's probably a pretty normal reaction." She looked around the room. "I saw Amanda leaving when I was coming. She said an odd thing to me, and I probably should listen to her, but you know me."

"What do I know about you?"

"That I'm honest to a fault."

Marnie really was. How could she have thought she couldn't be trusted? Where had that bizarre thought even come from? "I do know that, so just spit it out."

"Amanda told me not to mention the word reporting. Why? You love being a reporter, and I don't understand why you wouldn't take those two reporting assignments I tried to give you. They could be done from here. They were perfect for you." She took a deep breath and stared at Raven, waiting for a response.

Her friend—not a reporter, Raven reminded herself. "I can't explain it either. I really can't. I just know I'm done with being a reporter."

"Why? There's lots you can do without ever having to leave this room. And you are so talented, Raven. It's a God-given gift—if you believe in that kind of thing. It wouldn't be right not to use it."

"I don't know what to say. I just know I'm done being a reporter." She couldn't explain even to herself why the thought of being a reporter made her skin crawl.

Marnie sighed. "OK, well I'm not arguing about it. But we will discuss it again at a later time. When you're feeling stronger." Marnie reached over and patted her hand. "Let's talk about some happy things.

First, I emptied your apartment like Amanda asked me to do. All your stuff is in storage—waiting for you. Your landlord was very accommodating."

"He's a nice guy. Sent me a plant." She pointed at one on the windowsill.

Marnie reached in her basket. "And even gave you back your security deposit. That's your first gift. He even insisted on helping to load up the truck. And the second piece of good news is that you're still on our payroll which means you still have health insurance. So no worries there."

"But I'm not coming back to the paper."

"You never know what the future holds, but you were an employee at the time you went missing, and so you're staying on the payroll until you leave here. Of course, you won't get any pay, but you will get the insurance. When you're feeling better, we can talk about your future with the paper."

"Are you sure?"

"Very sure. And I brought you your favorite snacks and..." She reached back in the basket. "The piece de resistance. I know it's not your laptop, but I couldn't find it. This is Internet-capable so when you're ready to join the world, you can. I can't believe you don't even have a phone."

"I have a phone." She tapped the phone on her nightstand. "See."

"Hmph. I suppose. But you need to get a real phone so we can at least text each other. You know, keep in touch."

Raven couldn't meet her friend's gaze. "Maybe later."

"Sure when you're feeling better. So it must be nice to be near Amanda and her family."

Marnie was trying so hard to keep the conversation going. Raven wasn't. What was wrong with her? This was Marnie. Her friend. They'd shared so many secrets and laughs. And now Raven could barely talk to her. "I suppose, but I keep telling her she needs to spend time with her own family"

"I'm sure she doesn't mind. She's just thrilled that you're a…never mind."

"Alive. It's OK, Marnie. I know I almost died. And I'm struggling to be happy about the fact I survived. But right now, it's a little hard. Even with the meds, I'm in a lot of pain."

Marnie chewed on her lip. "I'm sure it is."

Raven wanted to scream and cry and tell her how unfair it all was. But there was no point in that. She was choosing powerful not pitiful. So she forced a smile. "Sorry for being so…so cranky."

"You're not being any such thing."

Raven really didn't want to talk about herself. "So, I guess you didn't find my laptop or my phone?"

"They weren't at your house or in your car."

"I'm sure I had them that night."

"I guess."

Raven remembered going back in her apartment to get it before she left to meet Marnie at the restaurant. She'd wanted to show… she sighed…to show her something. "I remember wanting to show you something that night. Did we discuss anything? About an upcoming story I was working on?"

Marnie shook her head. "Not really. You said you were working on something that might turn out to be big. Really big. But you always like to keep your projects secret. Even from me—your boss."

"I didn't give you a little clue?"

"Nope but…" Her friend stared off into space for a few moment. "Nope. Not a clue. I was trying to remember if you'd said anything. But I don't think you did. Still can't remember anything, huh?"

"Not a thing." Raven forced a smile. "But I keep telling myself that's probably for the best. Knowing what happened might be worse than not knowing. I'm just trusting that God knows what He's doing."

"Sounds like a plan, my friend."

Raven suppressed a yawn. "Thanks so much, Marnie. For coming and for taking care of the apartment for me. You're a good friend. I'll email you in a few days. After I get this thing set up on the new laptop. That was very kind of you."

Marnie apparently understood her hidden message. She stood up, looking uncertain. "No problem. I'm sure you're exhausted, but I wanted to see you with my own eyes. I…" She stopped talking then took a deep breath. "Somehow I feel like this is all my fault. You were coming to hang with me that night. If you weren't coming to meet me, then it might never have happened."

"Don't think that way. It's not your fault. It's that monster's—" She stopped. *Monster.* That word meant something.

"Are you OK, Raven?"

The almost memory disappeared. "Yeah, I'm fine."

"You got all pale and spaced out."

"You don't have to go. You drove all this way."

"I do if I want to get home before dark." She hugged Raven. "Remember ravens are one of the smartest animals, and they easily adapt to different environments. And so can you. You've got this."

Everybody kept telling her that. And each time

they did, she'd smile and agree, but the truth was she didn't have anything. But God did.

"I'll be back." Marnie smiled. "You get better, OK?" She waved as she went out the door.

Raven's gaze fell on the new laptop.

Marnie had said it would be wrong to not use her God-given gift. Writing had always been her passion, her dream. Just because she didn't want to be a reporter, didn't mean she couldn't write. Raven picked up the mini-laptop, and then opened a new file. She stared at the blank page for several long moments. She typed in the Bible verse that Gracie had given her and her thoughts on it. And then her fingers kept typing as if they had a mind of their own.

I can be pitiful or powerful, but I can't be both. I choose powerful.

10

Hunter Travis crawled through a cornfield on his stomach. The corn had already been harvested, and the remaining stalks didn't do much to keep them hidden. Which was why he was crawling.

"Tell me again why we're doing this?" Mark Williams whispered as he crawled behind him.

"Because I'm sure the man isn't Amish."

"Even though he was dressed Amish and drove home in a horse and buggy? I hate to tell you this. but nobody chooses to live without electricity or a car if they aren't Amish. The man is Amish."

"And what if he's not?"

"Each to his own I always say. Maybe he's in the process of converting. I'm sure that happens now and then."

"Probably. Sometimes I even think about it. There's a lot about their way of life that I find attractive. The simplicity. The way that everything revolves around their faith in God and their community. I wouldn't mind living like that."

"Yeah. It sure beats crawling around in a cornfield spying on people."

Hunter stopped crawling. They'd reached the end of the cornfield.

Mark crawled up beside him. "Now what?'

"Now we observe."

"That's it?"

"For now."

"You had me crawl around in the dirt in the dark just so we can lay here all night and watch?"

"I didn't ask you to come. You volunteered."

"Remind me not to do that again."

Hunter punched him in the arm. "You love this kind of stuff, so don't bother pretending that you don't."

"Whatever, man. Whatever. Does anyone else know we're here?"

"I texted the sheriff."

"What'd he say?"

"No idea. I was too busy following the buggy to read what he texted back."

"It's not like it was a speed chase. He was in a horse and buggy, and you were in a car."

"The law says don't text and drive, so I don't." Hunter pulled out his phone and brought up his text messages. "Boss says let him know what happens."

"Text him our location so they know where to come find our dead, frozen bodies when we don't show up for work in the morning." Mark chuckled at his joke.

"Good idea." Hunter sent the text and looked back at the house. The soft glow of light caught his attention. "That looks like lantern light to me."

"Yeah. So now that we're laying here doing nothing, would you mind explaining to me how we got here. Exactly."

"I was on a date."

"A date? Wow. That's a move forward for you."

"I figured it was time to get back on that horse."

"Anyone I know?"

"No. Not anyone I know either. It was a blind date. I guess not really a blind date. From a dating app. Met her at the hotel for dinner. Any way while we're eating this guy comes in, dressed in an Amish outfit but when he ordered his food—not one bit of an accent."

"And that caught your attention?"

"Wouldn't it catch yours?"

"Maybe, but I would have forgotten about it the next minute and paid attention to my date."

Hunter ignored the jab at his dating etiquette. "Something about him just didn't sit right with me. The more I watched him the more I knew something was wrong."

"So you ditched your date and called me to meet you? What did this date look like?"

"Quite beautiful. And I didn't ditch her. I paid for the dinner and escorted her to her car and thanked her for a lovely night."

"And a second date?"

"I don't think so. No chemistry. I got in my car, and the so-called Amish dude came out with his takeout orders. Several of them. That's another thing. When was the last time you saw Amish get takeout? That's when I thought I'd check him out. And then I called—" Something pressed against his back. Something that felt like a shotgun.

"What are you doing out here?"

"We're Holmes County Deputies. I have my identif—"

"I don't care who you are."

The shotgun pressed harder against his back. He

looked over at Mark. Another man held a shotgun against his back "Toss your weapons in front of you."

"What weap—"

"Now. Or I shoot."

Hunter pulled his gun from his shoulder holster and tossed it.

Mark did the same.

"Same with the phones."

When both men had done that, the one holding the gun on Hunter said, "Stand up. If you make any kind of move, I'll shoot you. And would be well within my rights since you're on my property. And I had no idea you were deputies. I thought you were going to rob me."

"He doesn't sound very Amish to me, Mark. What do you think?"

"I think you're probably right." Mark stood up to his full six-feet-four-inch height. He turned and faced the man. "If I were you, I'd put your weapon down. Before things get really bad."

The man laughed then pressed the gun against his chest. "Turn around and walk to the house. Both of you."

"How'd you know we were out here?" Hunter asked.

"Saw the lights from your phones. Next time you're trying to hide in the dark, I wouldn't use them."

Hunter said, "Good advice. I'll try to remember that next time."

"There won't be a next time for you two." The man pressed the gun harder into Hunter's back.

No one spoke as they made the trek to the house. Once inside, the man holding the gun on Hunter told the other man, "We'll put them upstairs in the empty bedroom. We'll take care of them later. Right now, we need to pack up so we can get out of here."

The man poked Hunter in the back. "Keep moving."

The kitchen table Hunter passed was filled with cellophane-wrapped packages. "Hey, Mark. It looks like we found that new distributor we've been hunting for."

"I think you're right."

Hunter turned toward the man with the gun. "You're under arrest. You have the right to—"

The man whipped the gun across his face. "Shut up. And move it. Next time, I'll shoot instead of hit. Get some rope. Or tape."

"Will do."

The man poked Hunter. "Up the steps. Both of you."

Hunter moved up the steps without comment. As they neared the bedroom door, he looked at Mark. "Now?"

"Now."

Hunter turned toward the man, and at the same time pulled back his fist. The man lifted the gun, but Mark grabbed it as it went off. The kick of the gun and Hunter's fist caused the man to fall backward.

"What's going on?"

Hunter looked at Mark. "Out the window."

By the time Hunter was in the room, Mark had opened the window and crawled through it. Footsteps pounded up the steps. Hunter climbed through the window and jumped.

He landed on his feet. A sharp snap and then his leg gave out. As he crumpled to the ground he yelled out to Mark. "Get the guns. I can't walk. Go."

Mark ran toward the cornfield.

People ran out of the house, yelling.

Hunter pressed against the house, praying. God, keep Mark safe. His family needs him. It was true. Mark's family did need him. Nobody needed Hunter. If somebody had to die tonight, it should be him. "Mark, keep running. Don't come back."

A few moments later, Hunter had three guns pointed at him. The original man from the restaurant stepped toward him. "It didn't have to be like this. You should have minded your own business."

"Just doing my job."

"Well, that'll get you killed." He pointed the gun at Hunter.

Sirens blared and red lights flashed from the road.

The men looked at each other.

One of them yelled, "Let's go."

They ran.

11

Mark walked into Hunter's hospital room. "Just like you to miss all the action. You drag me out to a cornfield, and then I have to clean up the mess."

"Yeah, you got to have all the fun. How many did you get?"

"Five, but they're singing like canaries, so I think by the time this is all said and done there will be a lot more arrests. Not just here but statewide."

"That's good."

"Thanks, man, for having my back. When they heard you yelling, they forgot all about looking for me. Gave me time to get to our guns. I was on my way back when the cavalry showed up."

"That was my plan."

"Brave thing to do."

"Nah, just doing my job."

"You had three shotguns pointed at you. That's a little more than doing your job."

"Speaking of the cavalry, how did the boss know to send them in?"

"He said his gut."

"Gotta love his gut, right?"

"I do now. Anyway, how's the leg?"

"Doctor says it was a clean break. It shouldn't

cause a whole lot of problems. Says it'll probably be a month or so before I get cleared for duty. But it will be limited duty for a while."

"So I guess that means you won't be able to teach your classes either."

"That's what it means."

"Oh, my, what will all your fans—I mean students, do without you?"

Hunter laughed. "What's your point?"

"I've said it before, and I'll say it again. I think those women just take the class so they can hang out with you."

"Are you saying I don't teach them anything?"

"Not at all, buddy, not at all. Anyway, Cindy told me to tell you that she expects you to come stay with us while you recuperate."

"That sounds just like your sweet wife but no can do."

"Why not?"

"It's already been arranged, I'm to be spending some time at Millersburg Rehab. That way I have someone to cook for me and take care of me plus get rehab. And it's all on the county dollar."

"Sounds pretty good. But are you sure? It's still a nursing home instead of a real home. Cindy really does want you to stay with us. We'll make sure we get you to rehab. It won't be a problem."

"I know that. But this way is better. Tell Cindy to visit and be sure to bring me some of her world-famous lasagna when she does."

Mark nodded. "That will make her a little happier. But you better make sure you tell her I begged and begged you to stay to our house. Or I won't be getting any of her lasagna."

"I'll be sure to tell her."

12

Sweat trickled down Raven's forehead. Her new haircut was plastered to her head. Her hands were on the parallel bars. She willed herself to stand up.

Her physical therapist said, "Use your arms to help."

She tightened her grip and pulled. Up. An inch. And then another inch. And then…back to her seat.

"Great job. Take a break, Raven."

"That wasn't a great job. I didn't stand all the way up."

"I didn't expect that you would. You worked hard. You deserve a break."

She shook her head. "No. I want to do this. I can do this. I can."

"You can and you will, but you've done plenty today. Drink a little water and take a short break. Then we'll start again."

"No. If we quit now, it just makes it harder to start again."

"OK. Five more minutes and then we're done for the day. Agreed?"

"Agreed."

"I'll put my arms around your waist to give you a little extra support. OK?"

"OK."

Martina put her arms around Raven's midsection. "Ready when you are. Take your time."

Raven took a deep breath and pulled herself upwards. One inch. Two. And then she was standing. Not by herself, but she was standing.

"Start counting."

"One. Two."

Martina removed one hand and then the other. Raven got to eighteen before she allowed herself to sit back down. "I did it."

"You did it."

Raven couldn't stop from crying. She looked up at Martina through her happy tears. "I will walk again, won't I?"

"Sure looks that way to me."

"Thanks so much, Martina."

"It's all you, Raven. I just tell you what to do. You're the one doing it."

"I can't wait to tell Amanda."

Martina stooped down so she was eye level with Raven. "Now, I mean this, and you better listen to me. You trust me, right?"

"Right."

"No trying to stand up on your own yet. If you try, you could undo all the hard work you've done up to this point."

"OK."

"Not just OK. Promise me."

Raven sighed. "I promise not to try to stand on my own until my wonderful physical therapist tells me I can. Happy, now?"

"Yes, I am. Now go have a good rest of the day. And don't forget to do your ankle pumps and isometric contractions at least two more times today."

"You are such a drill sergeant, but trust me, I won't forget. Thanks again, Martina." Raven turned her wheelchair around and headed for the door.

"You made that look easy."

Raven stopped.

The man talking to her was young. At least young compared to the other men in the nursing home. Actually probably about her age—at least in the same decade. "It was just about the hardest thing I've ever done."

"I didn't mean to insult you. I was just trying to find a way to talk to the most beautiful woman in the room."

"Don't bother. I don't talk to strangers." That wasn't true. She'd made a living talking to strangers. But not anymore. Her hands moved on the wheels to leave.

He held out his hand. "Then let's not be strangers. I'm Hunter Travis. And you are…"

"None of your business." She rolled several feet past him.

"Then I'll just call you Jane Doe."

She looked back at him. "Why?"

"That's what the police call an unknown woman. And if you won't tell me your name, then what choice do I have?"

"That has to be one of the worst pick-up lines ever." She rolled out of the room.

~*~

Way to go, Travis. Apparently, he'd lost his touch with women. It hurt a man's confidence when his fiancée called off the wedding a week before the blessed event without an explanation. That had been six months ago, and he was over it. In fact, he now saw that she'd been right, but he still hadn't found anyone he really liked. The few blind dates he'd been on had gone absolutely nowhere.

But this woman— even with her jet black hair plastered against her head and all sweaty from the physical therapy— this was a woman he'd like to get to know better.

Oh, well. It was obvious she didn't feel the same.

"You ready, Hunter?"

He rolled around to face his own physical therapy. "You betcha."

"I couldn't help notice you putting moves on my last patient. How'd that work out for you?"

"Not good. She wouldn't even tell me her name." He smiled. "But I bet you know it, don't you?"

"Ever heard of patient confidentiality?"

"But—"

"Time to work."

13

"Hey, sleepyhead."

Raven opened her eyes. "I'm not sleeping, Gracie. Just resting."

"OK if you say so. I always snore when I'm resting too."

She laughed. "OK, maybe it was a bit more than resting. Physical therapy tired me out today."

"You gave it your all, huh?"

"I did. I stood up. For a count of eighteen."

Gracie high-fived her. "Awesome, Raven. I'm proud of you. Anyway, I was thinking we could do Bible study in the conference room today. Unless you're not up to it."

"I'm up to it, but why?"

"I'm starting a new group today. I call it my Under Fifty group."

"That would leave out everyone but me."

"Not true, Raven. How about it?"

"I suppose. Give me a few minutes, and I'll meet you there."

"Want some help getting in your wheels? We can call an aide."

"Nah, I can do it. I'm getting to be an old pro at it."

"See you in the conference room."

"Be there in five."

Ten minutes later Raven rolled into the conference room. She looked around the room then at Gracie. "Really?"

She grinned and winked. "What? I told you that you weren't the only person under fifty in here."

"Hi, Jane Doe. I can't believe it. I get a second chance to get your name." He held out his hand. "In case you've forgotten. Mine's Hunter Travis."

"I actually had forgotten."

"That hurts, Jane. I usually have a more memorable impact on women. It must be because of this." He tapped his wheelchair. "But I'm in good company."

Raven looked at Gracie. "Well, I can see why we needed the conference room. Three wheelchairs take up a lot of space."

"It looks as though you two know each other, huh?" Gracie smiled.

"Not really." They both answered at the same time.

"Why did you call her Jane?"

Hunter laughed. "We sort of met in the physical therapy room, but she wouldn't tell me her name, so I called her Jane Doe."

"Hunter's a sheriff's deputy." Gracie nodded to Raven.

"That explains the Jane Doe thing."

"Don't forget to tell her how I'm a hero, Gracie. Stopped a huge drug ring. Of course, I did have a little help with that. But I had to jump out of a window." He tapped his chair. "And here I am."

"Really? That's how you broke your leg?" Raven

asked.

"It really is. So what happened to you?"

"I don't want to talk about it."

"Sorry. I didn't mean anything by it. My bad."

Gracie intervened. "Raven, you don't...never mind. Let's get started."

"Raven. That's your name?" Hunter gave her pleased smirk.

"It is."

"I love it. Glad to meet you, Raven. Or should I keep calling you Jane?"

"Raven's fine."

Gracie took charge of the group. "Great. Now that we're done with introductions, let's get started. Second Timothy 4:16."

Hunter rustled through the pages as if it were a competition. "Got it."

Gracie motioned for him to continue.

"The Lord will rescue me from every attack and will bring me safely to your heavenly kingdom. To Him be the glory forever and ever. Amen."

Raven met Gracie's gaze, sure that she'd chosen that verse for a reason.

"Read it again, please," Gracie said.

"The Lord will rescue me from every attack and will bring me safely to your heavenly kingdom. To Him be the glory forever and ever. Amen." Hunter's voice was warm and comforting.

Raven closed her eyes and listened to the words.

"Amen." Raven agreed with a soft whisper.

They spent a few minutes discussing the verse and then moved on to others.

Finally, Gracie raised her hands as if to ward off evil spirits. "Enough for today, class. See you both on

Wednesday. Unless either of you are too busy."

"Not me. I'll be here." Hunter grinned. "How about you, Raven?"

"I'll try to fit it in my schedule." She started to turn her wheelchair around.

"Hold up a minute, Raven. See you later, Hunter."

"Wow. I can take a hint."

Gracie grinned. "Good to hear. See you later."

Hunter left.

Gracie looked at Raven. "I want to talk with you for a moment. Please don't take this the wrong way, but I am your counselor."

"Counsel away."

Gracie blinked and ran her hands through her hair making it even more spiky. "I couldn't help but notice that you didn't tell Hunter what happened to you."

"I just met him. And it's not really any of his business."

"True, but I got the feeling that you're ashamed of what happened. You have no reason to be ashamed. You didn't do anything wrong, Raven. You're the victim. There's no shame in that."

"Are you sure about that, Gracie? Because I'm not. I don't know what happened, but people don't usually get kidnapped for no reason."

"So what? I'm sure you didn't mean to get kidnapped. And even if you did something that lead to it, it still wouldn't be your fault no matter what you did or didn't do."

"I suppose."

"The longer you keep all this hidden, the more shameful it will feel. Secrets have a way of doing that. Don't enshrine it. Don't build a brick wall around it letting the shame grow. Instead of letting it live in the darkness, let the light change it into a badge of honor."

A badge of honor? Tears filled Raven's eyes. "I can't imagine that ever happening."

"But it can. God gives us that promise in Romans 8:28."

"All things work for the good of those who love him. Yeah, I remember the verse." Raven wiped at a tear.

"I didn't mean to upset you. But I don't want the monster to win."

A chill travelled up her spine at the word. "I don't want the...the...monster to win either."

"Then be proud of yourself. Proud that you survived. Proud of all the work you're doing to get better."

"I'll try."

"You know what that movie character says about trying. Don't try—just do or don't do."

Raven grinned. "Point taken."

14

Someone knocked on Raven's door.

"Helloooo."

"What do you want, Hunter?"

He hobbled in using his cane. He'd graduated from the wheelchair a few days earlier. "I came to say good-bye. Now that I'm able to walk—sort of, I can go back home."

Home. Raven didn't even have a home to go back to. But that wasn't Hunter's fault. Over the past few weeks, she'd come to enjoy his company. She would miss him, not that she'd admit that to him. "You may be walking but you don't look all that steady. Better sit down before you fall down."

He flopped in the chair. "Thanks."

"When's the doctor saying you can go back to work?"

"I have an appointment with him for next week. Of course, I can't be out chasing the bad guys and being a hero just yet. But I can sit at a desk and fill out papers, so I'm hoping he'll give me the OK for desk duty then."

"Sounds like a plan."

"So what's your plan? You know when you get out of here?"

"I don't have one. It'll be months before I get out of here."

"Not true. I saw you yesterday. You walked without assistance."

"Yeah, two whole steps."

"That's two more than you could do last week."

"True."

"What did you do before your accident? I mean I assume you had an accident. I don't mean to probe."

She ignored the unspoken question and answered the spoken one. "I was a reporter for the Marietta newspaper."

"Cool."

"Really? Most police officers hate the press."

"I think that's an exaggeration. We just like honest portrayals, and I'm sure your stories were completely honest. If you lived in Marietta, what brought you to Holmes County?"

"Maybe you should be a reporter. You seem full of questions."

"Not trying to be nosy. I'm a cop. We ask questions even when we're not working." He shrugged. "Just making conversation. That's all."

"My sister lives in Millersburg. When I had my...my accident, we decided it would be best if I was closer to her. Make it easier for her to visit."

"So you did have an accident?"

Gracie's advice about not being ashamed rolled through her mind. She trusted Gracie. She met Hunter's gaze. "I don't know."

"What do you mean?"

No shame. Wear it like a badge of honor. "I don't know what happened to me. I can't remember."

"Oh, I'm sorry. I didn't mean to bring up bad

memories." He shook his head. "Oops. That's the wrong thing to say, isn't it? Let me try again."

"It's really OK, Hunter. Gracie says I need to talk about it. Not be ashamed of it."

"That sounds like good advice."

"How do you know that? You don't know what I'll say."

"Maybe not, but I know you—at least a little bit. And I can't believe that you've done anything to be ashamed of."

"That's sweet. If you have a minute, I'll tell you all about it. Or at least what I know about."

"I've got nothing but time."

She explained the circumstances in which she was found.

He listened.

"And that's it." She finished.

"See, I was right. I knew you hadn't done anything to be ashamed of."

"But you can't really know that for sure. I don't know what I did that lead up to what the police believe was a kidnapping."

"I can know that. Because no matter what you did, you didn't deserve to be kidnapped for months. And you certainly didn't deserve to be hurt the way you were hurt. Nobody deserves that."

"I suppose that's true. There's something else. I've wanted to talk to you about it anyway."

"You have?"

"Well, sort of. If I ever get out of here—"

"You mean when you get out of here."

"You're right, that's what I mean. When I get out of here, I want to take some self-defense classes. I want to be able to protect myself. Since you're a deputy, I thought you might have a recommendation."

"I absolutely do."

"Maybe you can get me their information."

"I can do that. Got a phone?"

She pointed to the nightstand. He picked up her new phone. After pressing in some numbers, his phone began to ring. He handed her the phone and answered his. "Hunter Travis here. Full time sheriff's deputy, and part-time self-defense instructor."

She laughed. "Are you kidding?"

He shut off his phone. "Not kidding. I teach at the local Y. Call me when you're ready. Thank you for talking with me. I've learned more about you in the last fifteen minutes than in the three weeks I've been here."

"It's hard for me to talk about myself. I guess that's what made me a good reporter. I'd rather let other people talk about themselves."

"And you will be again."

She shook her head, her voice adamant. "I don't want to be a reporter anymore."

"Why not? You said you were good, and you loved it."

"I was, and I did, but not anymore. I'm not sure why, I just know I never want to be a reporter again."

"That's OK. I'm sure you'll come up with an even better plan."

She grinned. "At least I have plenty of time before I have to decide."

"Not nearly as much as you think. Things happen fast once you reach certain points in therapy. Suddenly you can do things again." He stood up. "If it's OK with you, I'd like to stop in every now and then to check on you."

She hid her smile. "I guess that would be OK."

15

Hunter was right. Her release time came much sooner than she'd thought possible. She still didn't know what happened during her missing time, but with God's help she'd been able to move past the lost memories and look forward to the future.

First and foremost, she wanted to live a life that would honor God. For months after waking up in the hospital, life had been about her. Her pain. Her missing time. Her. Her. Her. It was only when she put the focus where it belonged—on God—that the long process of healing had really begun. Countless hours of therapy—physical and mental—as well as Bible study with Gracie, had brought her to this plan.

Raven was ready to start her life again. After six months, she was leaving the rehab center, finally. And she was walking out. Sure, she had to use a cane, but even that was temporary. She'd been cautioned by everyone to take things slow, though, so she intended to follow those orders.

She was still in recovery—a new stage but still recovering.

The second part of her plan included living in a small house in Charm that she and Amanda had found. Just as the name implied, it was a charming

Amish village and not too far from where Amanda lived, but far enough that the two wouldn't feel obligated to see each other every day. Raven didn't want to interfere in her sister's life.

The third part of the plan, the part she hadn't shared with anyone, was to finish the manuscript she'd been working on since the day Marnie gave her a new laptop. After that she'd have to find a publisher. When she'd started writing that day it was just a way to vent but it had turned into much more than that. It was part diary and part Bible study. She wanted to share with the world what she'd discovered—that God was all powerful, all good, but most importantly, all loving. And, oh, so faithful.

She wasn't sure what she'd do after the book was published, but she was sure God would reveal it to her when the time was right. And that was just fine with her. She had more than enough to do for now.

"All set?" Amanda walked in.

"More than ready."

"I still don't know why you couldn't just live with us for now. We have the room. And I really don't like the idea of you living so far away."

Raven laughed. "It's less than twenty minutes from your house. I used to live hours away."

"I still think it would be better if you lived with us. For now."

"I love you for making the offer, sis, but I think we both know we'd get on each other's nerves after about three hours. I'll be close enough to enjoy you and the family but far enough that you won't get sick of me. Trust me, this way is better."

"I think I should be insulted, but I'm not." Her sister fluffed her hair and tossed her head back.

"Anyway, your stuff arrived at the house. We arranged the furniture, but if you want to change it let us know. We can certainly do that. I bought you some groceries to get you through the first few days, so you don't have to run right out to the grocery store."

"You are an angel, Amanda."

Amanda smiled. "I'm not, but thanks for saying that. We didn't go through most of the boxes. We figured you'd want to go through that stuff on your own. But we put the boxes in the rooms marked on them. Marnie did a great job with organizing your things."

"That's why she's the boss. You are too good to me, Amanda." She looped her arm through her sister's. Even with the cane, she made Amanda skip a few steps with her. By the time they got down the hall, they were both laughing so hard they had to stop.

Once in the car, Amanda drove out of Millersburg past many farms and a few businesses.

One of the reasons Raven had chosen Charm was that it was off the beaten path. It wasn't even an incorporated town, although it did have a school, several businesses, and some tourist attractions. Just the sort of place where she could start life over.

Amanda pulled up in front of Raven's new home. Only one close neighbor. The other houses on the road were far enough away that it would take a few minutes to walk to them.

Raven stared at the house. It was the exact opposite of her apartment in Marietta. This looked like the all-American dream, a tiny, gingerbread cottage with a detached garage surrounded by a white picket fence. Someone had planted flowers that were in full bloom in spite of it only being March, including a beautiful red rose bush.

Amanda turned to her. "It really is a pretty place. I think you'll be happy here."

"I think you're right." Raven got out of the car, hobbled up the steps, and unlocked the door. "Did you see the deck out back?"

"It's awesome."

They walked inside.

Raven stared at the two flowery loveseats that had never quite fit the décor in her apartment. They were perfect here.

There were boxes everywhere. In the living room. In her bedroom. In the kitchen. She grinned at Amanda. "At least I won't be bored. It seems as if I have plenty to do."

"Just don't try to do it all in one day. And I did manage to get the cable on for you, so you can sit and relax. And make sure you do."

"OK, Mom." Raven walked out to the kitchen. "Let's see if you know how to shop for me."

A double-layer cake decorated with pink and red roses sat on the counter. Words were painted in the top.

Welcome Home!

Raven looked at her sister. "Perfect. I guess you do know what I like."

"As much weight as you've lost, you need to eat the whole thing yourself."

"You don't want a piece?"

"Of course I do. And a cup of coffee." Amanda pointed at the coffeepot on the counter. "I did manage to find that in the boxes."

When the coffee was ready the two of them walked out to the small deck. While the front yard had a white picket fence, this one had a wooden privacy fence. Raven could sit out here all day in her pajamas if she felt like it.

"I think you'll spend a lot of time out here." Amanda said as she sat down at the round picnic table.

They ate a few bites of the cake in silence, enjoying the calm atmosphere.

"So what are your plans?" Amanda asked. "Not that you need any plans right away. Just curious."

Raven hadn't told anybody about her book. For some reason, she wanted to keep the privacy of her thoughts exposed on paper to herself for now. "Well, first thing tomorrow I'm starting self-defense classes."

"Self-defense classes? Are you up to that physically?"

"I don't know, but I'm sure going to try. Nobody's ever kidnapping me again. At least not without me putting up a fight, anyway."

Amanda nodded.

"Then maybe I'll see if there are any jobs around here."

"Really? You're ready for a job?"

"I didn't say that I was ready. But I might look around. See if there's anything available."

"According to Marnie, your job's still waiting for you."

"I don't want to be reporter."

"I know. I just don't understand your attitude. You loved being a reporter."

"I don't understand it either, but it is what it is."

"Don't rush into any decisions. And you don't need to take any old job. Take your time."

"I will, sis. I will."

Amanda looked at her watch. "Better go if I'm to

beat the school bus home."

Raven stood up and hugged her sister. "I don't have the words to tell you how much I appreciate all you've done."

"Good. No need to tell me. We're family. That's what families do. I love you."

"I love you, too."

Amanda stared at her.

"What? Just say whatever it you want to say."

"Am I that transparent?"

"I always could read you like a book, and you know how much I love to read."

"Yes, I do. You know your counselor said you might have some issues adjusting. So if you need to talk you call me day or night. Promise. I can be here in fifteen minutes."

"Only if you speed. I'll be fine. Stop worrying about me."

Her sister's eyes filled with tears. "I know you're the one this happened to, but I was so sure I would never see you again. I'm...I'm...I just want you to understand you're not a burden to me. If you need me, you call. Got it?"

Raven hugged her, a little teary eyed herself. "Got it."

Amanda left.

Raven sat back down, looking out at her little yard feeling the sun's heat. Her mind and body relaxed, truly relaxed, for the first time in months. No façade, no pretending, no hyper-awareness that others were watching and expecting her to work things through.

Alone.

The first time she'd been truly alone in almost a year. Sure she'd had a private room at the rehab but people were only a buzz away if she needed them. But no more. She was on her own.

Raven wasn't sure how she felt.

She shook off the confusing, restless feeling and walked back in the kitchen. Seeing the cake made her stomach rumble, and she ate a few more bites. The boxes in the kitchen looked out of place, so she opened one. Working filled her mind. She went through boxes, sorted, and organized until bedtime. As she got ready for bed, a sense of uneasiness stirred.

Maybe this part of her plan wasn't as good as she'd originally thought. Amanda's idea of living with her family seemed more appealing as she walked through the house once again, double-checking the locks, for the third time. If anyone saw through the windows, the boxes showed someone was moving in or out. Perhaps giving the impression it was unoccupied.

Oh, well. Too late now. She crawled into her bed, knowing there was no way she'd sleep even though she was exhausted. It was too quiet.

And she was all alone.

16

In a barn. Chains around her ankle and her wrist. Raven wanted to scream but couldn't. She lay there not moving, terror washing over her like waves on a beach. She was too afraid to even open her eyes. Help me, God. Help me, God. Help me, God. I don't want to be here. Finally, her racing heart slowed, and she found the courage to open her eyes.

Not in a barn. But in a bed—her bed in her bedroom in her own house. In Charm, Ohio. Safe. Nobody was hurting her. Raven laid there, still not moving. She touched the cotton sheets. The quilt. They felt real. But that barn felt real, too. She could almost smell it.

Her hands clutched the cotton sheet. I'm safe. I'm safe.

Birds chirped outside her window.

Just a dream—more like a nightmare. It was to be expected her first night in a new house alone. Raven sat up allowing time to acclimate to this new reality. A sunny March morning in Charm, Ohio in her own house. She took a deep breath—then understood why she'd dreamt about a barn.

She wasn't in Marietta now.

She was in horse country with all the lovely scents

Lillian Duncan

associated with it. She peeked out the window. A horse and buggy was in her neighbor's drive. No wonder she dreamt about a barn.

Raven walked to the kitchen, ignoring all the boxes she still needed to go through. She would have plenty of time to do that. She poured a glass of milk. She was still taking a few meds because of pain but it was getting better.

Her small deck was inviting, and she sat down with a piece of cake to go with the milk.

Birds chirped.

This house was so perfectly adorable but so different from her life in the city. Would she miss a place without restaurants and museums? She wasn't sure. But for now, this seemed a much better fit for her. She was renting right now, but if her plan worked out, she might just buy the place. If she liked living in Charm. No quick decisions. Just one day at a time.

As Raven listened to the birds, she couldn't get that dream out of her head. She rubbed her wrist; she could almost feel the chain around it. Maybe it wasn't just a dream but a memory.

Her doctors had said she could recover her memories at any time. Could that barn and the chains have really happened? She closed her eyes, trying to remember. But if it was a memory, it was gone now.

It was time to get moving. She went in the house, found her phone, and dialed the number.

A deep male voice answered, "Hello."

"Is this Hunter Travis?"

"It is."

"This is Raven Marks. From rehab." She hadn't seen him since he'd left, though he'd asked to stop by. But she didn't care about being his friend—she needed a self-defense instructor.

"How are you, Raven? I've been thinking about stopping in to see you, but I've been so busy."

"Not a problem. I'm still interested in setting up some self-defense classes with someone. If you're too busy, maybe you can suggest someone else."

"Are you out of rehab already?"

"Moved out yesterday."

"That's awesome. I told you it wouldn't take as long as you thought. I actually have some time open today."

"Perfect."

An hour later, Raven walked out to the garage. She stared at her car. The last time she'd been in it, something bad had happened. Maybe she should trade it in? But she really didn't have extra money for a new car right now. Still she sort of hated it.

Pitiful or powerful?

She chose powerful and opened the car door. Her purse and insulated lunch bag, with two bottles of water and a can of soda, went on the passenger side floor. Martina had told her after exercise to keep hydrated. She wasn't sure what the gym would offer, so she decided to bring her own.

At the Millersburg Fitness Center, she walked up to the reception desk. "I'm looking for Hunter Travis."

"Right behind you, Raven." He grinned as she turned. "You look great. And walking on your own. That's awesome. I don't want to, but I have to say I told you so."

"Yes, you did."

"How's the pain?"

"It's OK. I have some, but it's getting better every day."

"Want to sit down?" He motioned at two chairs. "Let's talk for a few minutes before we start the session."

She nodded, suddenly self-conscious as her cane clicked on the floor. Her cheeks warmed. She forced a smile as she sat down.

"I want to apologize. I asked if I could stop by and visit and then I never did."

"No apology needed. I know picking up with one's life can be hectic until one gets it all sorted out."

"Still, I'm sorry. I really meant to stop by." His apologetic expression was sincere. "So, what are your goals for your sessions with me?"

"I want to be able to protect myself. Plain and simple."

"Are you still in physical therapy?"

"Once a week but she thinks that should only be for another month or so."

"Is it OK with Martina for you to take self-defense classes? I'll need a written release from her."

She pulled a paper out of her purse. "Here it is."

"You came prepared."

"I did. I know I'm not ready to do all the hard stuff, but I wanted to get started right away. I want to be able to defend myself if I need to."

"Still no memory?"

Had the dream been a memory? She couldn't say for sure. "No."

"Sadly, there are a lot of bad people out there. And even in our small town there's more bad people than most folks realize."

Not just bad people. Monsters. A chill went down her spine. That word meant something, but what?

"OK. The first thing you need to know about self-defense is to always leave a situation that feels wrong. Trust your instincts. If it feels wrong, leave. No matter where you are, who you're with, or what you're doing."

"Leave? I want to be able to defend myself."

"I agree, and we'll work on that, but truly the best defense is to leave situations that don't feel safe. It's better to err on the side of caution. If you're wrong, so what? But if you're right, you've stayed safe."

"That makes sense."

"And the second thing is that you need to be as healthy and strong as you can be."

"What's that mean?"

"It means that before you start to learn any self-defense moves, you need to work on getting stronger. In other words, an extension of the physical therapy you've been doing."

That wasn't what she had in mind at all. "I want to be able to take a man down if he tries to hurt me. Give him a karate chop or something."

He laughed. "I understand. But it's important for you to be strong enough to get away from him if the situation calls for it."

They stared at each other.

Hunter grinned. "It's up to you. I'm sure you can find someone else to help you. But if you want me to help you, we have to do it my way."

"And what exactly is your way?"

"Strength, flexibility, and endurance, first. When I feel like you're ready we can talk about some of those karate chops."

"Fine. I'll do it your way."

~*~

Raven's whole body was shaking as she sat down on a chair on her front porch. The session with Hunter was far more strenuous than she'd expected. He'd had her walk a mile, made her use some weights, and then they'd done stretching exercises at the end. She sipped on the cola from her bag, glad she'd thought ahead on that score and hoping the sugar and caffeine would revive her.

"Hello." An older Amish lady stood on her side of the driveway holding a plate.

"Hi."

"I just wanted to welcome you to the neighborhood." Her German accent was slight, making the *J* in "just" come out as "chust."

"That's so nice. Thank you."

"My name is Lydia." She crossed the drive and climbed up the steps.

"My name is Raven. I hope you don't mind if I have one right now. That's why I'm sitting here. I'm a little shaky."

"Oh, my. Of course not." She passed that plate of cookies to Raven. "Eat as many as you want. I have more in the house. I like a cookie every now and again, so I made two batches."

Raven's hand shook as she picked up a cookie and munched on it. She took a deep breath. "That's better, I think."

"Do you need a doctor?"

"No. I just overdid it a bit. I was working out. I'll be smarter next time." Hunter would have to take it down a notch or two. She picked up another cookie.

"So, how are you liking Charm so far?"

"It's seems perfect. I wanted a place that was quiet."

"It is quiet, not as quiet as living on a farm. But I do enjoy living here. I moved into town after my husband passed. There was no reason for me to stay out on the farm alone. Too much work for one person."

"Couldn't your children help?"

"Sadly, God did not bless me in that way."

"Oh, I'm sorry. I didn't mean…"

"Not a problem. It was God's will. And I love living in town. I can walk to the store and to the restaurant. And my friends come to visit me quite often."

"Was that your buggy I saw this morning?"

"No. A friend stopped by. I don't have a buggy any longer. No place to keep the horses. I have a three-wheeler bicycle for town, and then I hire someone if I want to go to Millersburg or Berlin."

"If you ever need to go somewhere, let me know. I'll be glad to take you. I'm not working right now, so I have plenty of time."

"That is so very nice of you, Raven."

Raven held up the cookies. "This was very nice of you."

Lydia smiled. "It was my pleasure. I will bring you over some more."

Raven looked down at the plate. Almost empty. "That's not necessary."

"True, but I will, chust the same."

17

"So how are you? Really?" Gracie ran her fingers through her hair.

Raven still had weekly sessions with Gracie after her physical therapy session. They were part therapy and part Bible study. She sighed. "Good and bad."

Gracie laughed. "OK, you can't give me an answer like that without an explanation. More please."

"It's just different. When I was here, I didn't have to worry about my future but now...I have to figure out what to do with the rest of my life."

Gracie gave her a penetrating look. "I can understand that, and I'm sure you'll figure it out. But there's no rush. You really are still in recovery. Keep praying. God will give you answers. But I don't really think that's what the good and bad answer was about. Is it?"

Raven tried to meet Gracie's gaze but failed. "Probably not."

"So what's really going on?"

"I'm afraid."

"Of what?"

"Everything." Raven shuddered. "I feel so weak admitting that. When I'm with other people, I'm OK but when I'm alone I just get scared."

"Oh, sweetie. That makes sense after all you've been through."

"I guess. Except I don't really know what I've been through." She shrugged. "Understanding doesn't make it any easier."

"I suppose not. So have you been continuing Bible study on your own?" Gracie had a way of leading things—everything—back to God.

"Not really."

"I thought not." He fingers tapped the side of her wheelchair as she stared off into space. "Too busy?"

"I can't really use that as an excuse. The truth is I just didn't think about it. But I do keep reminding myself that I'm powerful not pitiful."

"That's good. I'm not reprimanding you. Your life—your choices. Buuuuut…"

"But what?"

"I can't tell you what will work in your life. That's between you and God. But I can tell you what worked—what still works every day in my life. It's the Bible. It's as simple as that. God's Word is power. Power to overcome. Power to more peace and joy. Power to turn your ashes into beauty."

"You sound so positive about that."

"I am. When I skip a few days of Bible study, I start to feel sorry for myself. And it takes no time at all for that to spread to every area of my life. I start feeling anger at my situation. And then hopelessness starts. And it just keeps getting worse. As soon as I start meditating on God's Word, it starts getting better."

"You think reading the Bible will help me stop being afraid?"

"When you put your trust in God, He is always faithful. There's a verse in Romans that talks about renewing your mind. The thing is, renewing your mind isn't a one-time thing. It's an ongoing process. I can't explain how or why but there is power in God's Word."

"OK, I'll start today. As soon as I'm done with my self-defense classes. If you can call it that. Hunter keeps telling me the best defense is to run away from a bad situation. It's more of a workout than a self-defense class."

"But I can see a difference in your walking so it must be helping."

"I guess, but I'm sure not admitting that to Hunter. Want to go out to dinner Friday night?"

"Sounds like a plan."

Raven stood. "See you then." She went to the door.

"And don't forget, Raven," Gracie said. "One of the most powerful things we can do is to be thankful and give praise."

"Count my blessings, right?"

~*~

"This is not what I had in mind when I said self-defense classes."

Hunter smiled as he jogged past her. "I know but as I always say…"

"The best defense is to run away. I get it. But I can't run."

"That's OK. Walk as fast as you can."

Making her voice louder since he was ahead of her on the track, she said, "I'm trying. I'm doing my best."

He turned and ran backwards. "Are you really?"

"I said I was."

"Don't believe her." Amanda yelled as she jogged onto the track. She'd joined in the classes a few days back. "She's never liked to run or do anything physical. There isn't a physical challenge she hasn't run from. Walking to the library and back is her idea of a workout."

"I suspected that all along. Good to know I was right."

Amanda ran past her.

"I'm glad you two enjoy tormenting me."

"It's what I get paid to do." He turned around and ran past Amanda. Within a few minutes he ran past Raven for the second time and then stopped. He threw her a towel. "OK. You can stop. Time to do a little strength training and then we'll practice the move I taught you last time."

She wiped the sweat off. "I'm exhausted."

"Nah—you just think you are. Proverbs 23:7 says you are what you think you are. So stopping thinking exhausted and start thinking you are strong and energetic."

Amanda ran past. "I'm doing two more laps and then I'll be over."

"See Amanda's thinking strong and energetic."

"She's always been like that. I wish I were more like her," Raven said as they walked toward the weight room. "But don't tell her I said that."

"Don't compare yourself to her, Raven. Besides you're doing great. I know I tease you, but I've seen great improvement since we started."

"Yeah, great improvement. I can walk around the track twice."

"Your walking is picking up speed."

By the time they finished the weights, Amanda walked in just in time for the self-defense part of the class. "OK, class. First rule of self-defense is…"

"Leave the situation." Amanda blurted out before Raven could. Her sister smiled pleased to have beaten her.

"And the second rule?"

"Never let them take you to a secondary location." Amanda blurted out again.

"I knew those answers too."

"Sure you did, sis. Sure you did." Amanda giggled.

"I'm sure you did, Raven. Now, here's a move that's guaranteed to protect."

Good. That's what she wanted—needed. Something that would make sure she never got kidnapped again. She waited.

"Someone grabs you by your arms. Whatcha going to do?"

The two sisters looked at each other, shrugged, then looked back at Hunter.

"One choice is to kick them in the groin."

"That's a great idea." Raven said.

Hunter shook his head. "Not a great idea."

"Why not? That's where men are most vulnerable, right?"

"I'm not going to argue that one, but there's a better option. When you move your leg up to kick them in the groin, you're going to lose your balance and either fall or waste valuable time trying not to fall. Plus he could grab your leg and you'd definitely fall."

Raven visualized just such a situation and realized he was right. "Then what should you do?"

"Kick them in the knee. As hard as you can. It can

be just as disabling to your attacker and it gives you time to…"

"Run away." Raven said then grinned at Amanda. "Beat you."

"You can kick anyway you can but if you can with the sole of your foot that would be the best. Let's practice but don't actually kick each other."

They took turns with each other and with Hunter.

"I suppose that move could help but not if he had a gun. Maybe I should just get a gun. Learn how to shoot."

"That's a horrible idea." Amanda said. "Maybe you should just move in with us if you're that afraid. We have plenty of room. And the girls would be thrilled to have their aunt living with them."

"I agree with Amanda. A gun is a terrible idea, but if you want, I can come over to your house and help make it safer. And maybe find a security company to install some safety features."

"Any security company would be too far away from Charm to help."

"I can at least come over and take a look at your house. See how we can make it safer."

"I don't want to impose."

"You're not. I volunteered, remember? I'll call you later to set that up," Hunter said. "OK, one slow lap around the track to cool down."

They all headed back out to the track.

As they were leaving, Amanda looped her arm through Raven's. She leaned in and whispered, "He's so cute and he's got a thing for you."

"Don't be ridiculous." Raven giggled. "But he is cute."

"I'll say. That curly brown hair, and those

smoldering brown eyes. If I weren't married, I'd go after him."

"I'm not going after anyone."

"That's OK. He's going after you. And that's even better."

"He's doing no such thing."

Amanda lowered her voice imitating Hunter. "I'll come over to your house and check it out." Then in her normal voice, "The only thing he's checking out is you."

"Don't be ridiculous." But Raven laughed. She couldn't help but be a little pleased.

~*~

The two sisters left arm in arm. They were whispering and giggling. It was nice to see Raven that way. When she first came to Hunter for lessons, she was so serious, so quiet. But she was changing. Not just physically but in other ways. She seemed to be healing even though she still felt weak and powerless and afraid. Dear Heavenly Father, Bless her. Give her back her peace and joy. Then he added as an afterthought, Bless Amanda, too.

As he drove to the sheriff's department for his shift, he still had Raven on his mind. What was that about? But he couldn't pretend he didn't know the answer. She was beautiful and sweet. But she was in no condition for a relationship. Not that he was looking for one anyway. He hadn't been involved with anyone since his fiancé had broken their engagement.

After the last woman he dated told him he had

trust issues, he'd decided she was right. If a person couldn't trust, there was no point in dating. One broken heart in a lifetime was enough for him. Raven might be beautiful, but he wasn't looking for a relationship.

18

Raven's fingers shook as she typed the words, *The End*. Her eyes filled with tears. She'd done it. She'd written a book, which she'd titled *Overcoming*. She didn't know what would happen now but just finishing it was a victory.

Even when she'd been a reporter, she'd always known someday she'd try her hand at writing a book. She'd assumed it would be fiction, but she'd been wrong. She stared at the words once again.

What an awesome feeling!

A few days later, Raven drove to Cleveland to meet with an agent. When she'd made the appointment, she hadn't told the secretary about the manuscript. Instead, she'd told her she was a reporter for the *Marietta Times*—which technically she still was—and she'd like to talk about what it was like to be an agent.

Raven walked into the agent's office without a cane. Another victory. She'd had many since leaving the nursing home. Physically and spiritually. After taking Gracie's advice about studying specific Bible verses about peace and joy, she thought she was finally overcoming the all-consuming fear.

A woman looked up from the computer screen.

"Can I help you?"

"I have an appointment with Julie Dunn. I'm Raven Marks."

"Go on in."

Raven walked into another office.

The woman stood up and shook her hand. "I'm Julie Dunn."

After introducing herself, Raven pulled out her manuscript, printed and bound. "I know I told your secretary I was looking for information about being an agent. And that's true, I'm planning on writing an article about your profession. But it wasn't completely true. I have a story."

Julie's eyes widened. "That's not how it's done. First, you send a query, and if I'm interested, then a proposal."

"I know that, and I'm sorry for blindsiding you. I'm hoping you'll at least read a few pages now. And if you're not interested, I won't waste your time. I'll ask you a few questions and then write an amazing article about you. I promise."

Julie sighed. "You're here, so I might as well. Please sit down."

Raven sat. She'd chosen this agency in Cleveland not just because it was close to Charm but because it was a Christian agency with a wonderful reputation.

Julie turned the first page and then more. Fifteen minutes later, she looked up. "This is a true story?"

"I wish it wasn't, but yes, it is."

"It's an incredible story and you know how to tell it. You're writing is not only captivating but clear and concise."

"I really am a reporter. Or at least I was before all that happened to me."

"It shows in your writing. If you can verify the story, I think this would be something I'd definitely be interested in representing."

"Not a problem. I included a list of people at the back who can verify specific events. My doctors. The rehab center. The sheriff's department that found me. I included a photocopy of the missing persons report. Things like that. There's just one condition I have."

She arched an eyebrow. "Really? Most writers are so happy to be published they don't give me conditions."

"I'm not trying to be difficult, and I really do want my story told. I think it could help other people. But my condition is that I don't want it published under my name. I want it to be published under the name, Jane Doe."

"Interesting. Why Jane Doe?"

"Because the story isn't about me. It's about God."

"So what happens if the book gets a lot of attention, because I believe it will? Are you willing to do interviews on TV? The publisher will want that—will insist on it, actually."

"As long as I can remain anonymous, I will."

"Again, why?"

"I really don't want my face shown on TV or my real name involved. After all, I really don't know what happened to me or who's responsible. I feel safer to stay anonymous."

Julie nodded. "So you're afraid? I suppose that makes sense."

"That's part of it. The other part is that I want to live a simple life. Not in the limelight. I'm not seeking celebrity." You're a self-centered, celebrity-seeking narcissist. The thought came out of nowhere. She ignored it and focused on Julie.

"Then why write the story at all?"

"That's a good question. The answer is there are so many people out there, hurting and broken. I want them to know that God loves them, and He will lift them out of their pit if they let Him."

Julie nodded. "And God lifted you out of that pit?"

"A little more every day."

"I'll focus on the safety factor with the publisher. In the end, I'm sure they'll agree to keeping you anonymous."

"Exactly how would that work?"

"They'd have to interview you without showing your face and perhaps disguising your voice. In fact, I think the publisher will love it. Built-in publicity. Should be magic with your excellent writing and an amazing story. I'll not have any problem selling this book. But I'd like to finish reading it before I offer you a contract. Is that OK with you?"

"Of course."

"You won't be going to any other agents or publishers out there while I'm reading it?"

"Not at all. I did my research, and you're the only agent I wanted to contact. I'm driving home when I leave here and that's where I'll be until I hear from you." She stood up. "My contact info's in there."

"Excellent." Julie stood and held out her hand. "I'm looking forward to working with you."

"Same here. Is there any place nearby that would be good for lunch before I go?"

"Do you like corned beef sandwiches?"

"Love them."

Julie stepped around the desk. "Let's go. My treat.

It's a great place and they have the most amazing sandwiches."

After lunch, Raven drove back to Charm. She had to keep wiping the happy tears away. She'd always wanted to write a book. And now she had. Just as Gracie said, when one put their trust in God He would turn ashes into beauty. She hated the reason for the book but loved the fact that she'd actually written it.

After using the remote to lock the garage door—one of Hunter's recommendations—she walked over to Lydia's. "You look busy."

Lydia had a hoe in her hand. "I decided to have a little garden this year. Just a few tomato plants and some peppers. My two favorite summer crops."

"Couldn't you find someone with a rototiller to plow it up for you?"

"Oh, I'm sure I could but a little hard work is good for the body, you know." She patted her ample stomach.

"So true." She held up the remainder of her lunch. She'd only been able to eat about a third of the sandwich. "I better get this in the refrigerator before it spoils."

~*~

Raven could smell the horses from her favorite spot on her deck. Actually not the horses, but their unpleasant by-product. She'd gone for a walk and accidently stepped in a pile by the roadside. She'd scraped her shoes on the grass, but some of the horse droppings still tracked from her shoes onto the cement walkway to her front porch. It stank, even though she'd removed her shoes and gone out to her back deck.

She sat at the picnic table with a Bible and index cards. Enough. She couldn't concentrate on God's Word with that nasty smell.

She went to the laundry room and grabbed a jug of bleach and a scrub brush. A chill went down her spine as she stared at them. She shrugged it away and walked out to her front walkway. She poured bleach on the offending mess then bent down with the scrub brush. The odor rushed up to meet her.

Everything turned wavy. She looked down at the walkway. It was gone.

Horse. Bleach. A cement floor, much larger than her walkway. She was back in the barn.

"So you're finally up. I guess I know where the Lazy Susan got its name."

"My name...not Suzie."

"It's whatever I want it to be. And I say it's Suzie Q." The monster paused for a moment. "Open your eyes." He paused. "You really are disgusting, you know that, Suzie Q? I mean really, Suzie Q? Don't you have any pride? You're filthy. And this place smells horrible. I think it's time for a good spring cleaning, don't you?

"Clean this place up. I'll take out the straw. If you do a good job, I might let you take a bath too. What are you waiting for? I said clean this mess up."

She collapsed. What was happening to her? She looked at her wrists. Thick heavy chains. And on her ankles. She curled up in a fetal position. She was back with the monster.

"Raven. Raven." Someone shook her. "Are you all

right?"

Not the monster's voice.

She opened her eyes.

Lydia was staring at her. Lydia. Her friend. Her neighbor. Not the monster. "Should I call for a doctor for you? Are you hurt? Did you fall?"

Raven shook her head, trying to reorient herself. This was real. Not the monster. Not the barn. "I'm all right, Lydia."

"You chust don't look all right." Lydia helped her stand.

"I'm...I'm not sure what happened." Raven looked around. She was back on the cement walkway that went to her porch. "I got dizzy, and then here you are."

"Let me help you get back to your house. And then I'll clean up this mess for you."

"That's not necessary. I'm OK. Really."

"I'm sure you are. But I'll help you back to your house chust the same."

Raven didn't argue. She was shaking so badly she wasn't sure if she could make it without some help. She leaned against Lydia and the two of them made it up her steps and into the house.

Lydia walked her to the sofa. "Would you like water or something with sugar? I'm thinking maybe you should have your sugar checked. You might have the diabetes, yes?"

"Sugar might be a good idea. I have soda in the refrigerator."

A moment later, Lydia was back.

Raven took a long sip from the can.

"This is not the first time you've had this shakiness. You should talk to your doctor, yes?"

She wanted to tell Lydia that it had nothing to do with diabetes and everything to do with being kidnapped, but fear stopped her. What would Lydia think if she knew the truth about her? Had it been a real memory or just a hallucination? Had the head injury done more to her brain? "It might be a good idea. I have an appointment in a few weeks. I'll let him know then."

"This is good." Lydia stood up. "Now, I will go out and clean that stinky mess."

"That's OK. I'm not sure why the smell bothers me so much." Or did she? "But it does. I'm sure I'll get used to it."

"Not to worry. I'll take care of it." Lydia left.

Raven leaned back against the sofa. She thought back to the first morning here. She'd dreamed of being in a barn. In chains. And now this. It couldn't just be her imagination, could it? It had been too real.

A memory.

Had she been chained in a barn? She could feel the heaviness of chains around her wrist, her ankle. And a man kicking her. Yelling at her. She was on her knees, scrubbing the floor with bleach.

She closed her eyes. The memory seemed so real. Just her imagination? Or a nightmare? But people didn't have nightmares when they were awake, right? She could remember being on her knees scrubbing. Smelling bleach and horse. And the man kicking her. What else had he done to her?

Maybe that was the real reason she couldn't remember anything. Maybe she didn't want to know what the monster had done to her. Monster? She remembered calling him that. He'd only laughed at her. He didn't seem to have been bothered to be called that.

"All done."

Raven opened her eyes. She wasn't in the barn. She was in her home. In Charm. And she was safe, wasn't she?

Lydia held the jug of bleach and the scrub brush. "Where do you want these?"

"In the kitchen is fine. Thank you so much for helping me."

"And you are feeling better, yes?"

Raven smiled. "Yes."

"Would you like me to make you lunch? You should eat something."

"I'm fine. I had a huge lunch." She stood up to show Lydia that she was better. With shaky knees, she walked over and hugged the older woman. "Thanks so much for helping me."

After Lydia left, Raven stood in the middle of the room, not sure what to do. Should she call Amanda or Gracie to tell them? Maybe if she talked to someone she'd remember more.

Not yet.

It was too fragile. Too personal. Too humiliating. A deep sense of shame filled her being. Did she even want to remember more? Her stomach clenched. She didn't want anyone else to know. What would they think of her? Being chained like a dog. How had she let that happen to herself?

She walked out to the kitchen. Staring at the bleach and the brush, she took a step toward them. And then another. She opened the lid, letting the scent of the bleach fill the kitchen. She took a deep breath and closed her eyes.

Nothing happened.

The memories would come back or not.

I trust you, God. You decide.

She looked at the clock. Today was her afternoon self-defense class with Hunter, but she wasn't up to it. These new memories had rocked her more than she cared to admit. She called Hunter. He didn't answer so she left a message. "Hunter. This is Raven. I'm not feeling well today. I'm sorry to give you such short notice but I'm canceling. See you next time. Thanks."

Bone-deep exhaustion overwhelmed her. She plopped onto the sofa and reached for her Bible.

~*~

The doorbell buzzed.

Raven popped up, startled, her Bible sliding from her chest into her lap. It took a few moments to orient herself. She was on her sofa, in her home. Safe and snug. She took a deep, fortifying breath and let it out. Probably Lydia checking on her.

She walked over and opened the door. "Hunter, I didn't expect you."

He held out a bowl. "Soup for what ails you. Homemade."

"Who made it? Your girlfriend?" She took the bowl.

"I don't have a girlfriend at the moment. And I made it. You know there are men in this world who can actually cook."

"Sorry, I didn't mean to be sexist." She stepped back. "Come on in."

"Did you eat dinner?"

"Not really."

"Good." He took the bowl from her. "You sit and I'll take care of you since you're the one not feeling well. Be back in a few."

Raven felt odd sitting on the sofa while Hunter did whatever it was he was doing in her kitchen. She stood up and then sat back down several times, not sure what to do. Finally, she went to join him.

"Hey, you're supposed to be resting."

"I've been resting all afternoon."

"Soup's ready."

Her stomach rumbled at the delicious smell. "I just realized I am hungry. How about we sit outside on the deck?"

"Sounds good. You lead the way."

She held open the door while he carried out the tray.

He grinned. "I haven't actually eaten yet either, so I brought enough for both of us, if you don't mind."

He placed a bowl of soup in front of her along with a saucer with rolls and a glass of water.

She looked at the soup. "I thought it would be chicken soup."

"Oh, nothing so mundane for this cook. I hope you like broccoli and cheese soup."

"Love it."

"I put Amish noodles in it. It puts it over the top."

She took a bite and gave him a thumbs up. "Delicious."

He ate several bites and then looked at her. "So what's up?"

"I…uh…" She didn't want to lie, and she didn't want to tell him the truth.

He grinned. "Never mind. It's OK if you don't

want to tell me. I shouldn't have asked. That's the cop in me. Always asking questions. Sorry."

"It's not that. I'm just not sure how to answer you." She took another bite and grinned. "This soup really is good."

"Nice change of subject, Raven. I have something else I wanted to talk to you about anyway. That's one of the reasons I stopped by. I wanted to tell you in person."

"That sounds serious. And mysterious."

"It's not that big of a deal. And I'm not being mysterious at all. My life is an open book."

She wished she could say the same. "OK, so…"

"Today's session would have been the last you paid for."

"Oh, I know. I'd planned to pay for another month today." She stood up. "Let me get my checkbook right now."

He put his hand on top of hers. "No. You're misunderstanding me. I don't want another check from you."

She sat down. "Am I that bad of a student? You think I'm hopeless? I know we've had to take it slow but I'm getting stronger every session. You said so yourself."

"It's not that at all."

"Then what is it."

He squeezed her hand. "It's a conflict of interest."

"What do you mean?"

He squeezed her hand again. "I don't want your money because I want to be your friend. Friends don't take money from friends."

"Oh…I see." Did he mean friends or more than friends? Her cheeks warmed. Which one did she want it to be? "I don't know what to say."

"That's OK. I've been practicing so I'll do the talking."

She smiled. This big, tough police officer and martial arts instructor was admitting he was nervous enough to practice what he wanted to say. She started to speak but he held up a hand.

"I want us to be friends, but I'm not looking for a relationship with anyone. I don't know about you, but I can always use another friend."

So that was it. Just friends. She ignored the sense of disappointment, but she couldn't blame him. Why would anyone want to be in a relationship with her? After the things that monster probably did to her. She forced a smile. "Friends sounds good."

"And friends don't take money from friends."

"They do if they're providing a valuable service for them."

He shook his head. "Not going to happen, Raven. We can keep up the sessions but no money's changing hands."

"That's not fair to you. Your time is valuable."

"Not as valuable as a friendship."

"But—"

"Those are my terms. Take them or leave them."

"You're being stubborn."

"It's one of my faults, but it's also an asset."

"It just doesn't seem fair to you."

"It's what I want. Besides, I'm fine, financially speaking. I have my job as a police officer. I don't do the martial arts things for money. It's a passion. You won't be the first person I gave free lessons to."

"Oh…" She arched a brow at him. "What do you do? Give every single woman free lessons?"

He laughed. "Not exactly. The last group I gave free lessons to was a group at the senior citizen center."

"Oh. Fine."

"Whyyyy....were you jealous?"

She grinned. "Not in the least, Hunter. After all, we're just friends."

19

Raven sat on her sofa flipping through the channels. When she came to the nightly news she stopped. It had been months since she'd bothered with the news. There'd been a time when the news was her obsession as well as her profession. But she no longer had the desire to hear about the pain of others. It only made her heart hurt, now that she understood suffering.

The news anchor was reminding everyone of the presidential primary debates that night. Funny, she hadn't even thought about the election for months. As a reporter, politics had been one of her assignments. It had been her secret dream to end up in Washington so she could be in the thick of it. In fact, she'd just finished a series on presidential hopefuls when she'd disappeared. How many of her profiled people had already dropped out of the race? Had her series even ran? Had there been any reaction to it? Maybe she'd watch a little of the debate—just to see what was happening. She wanted to remain an informed citizen voter.

Her life had become so small. It was about her and the few people she'd let in. Including Hunter—just as a friend, of course. She might have wanted more but he'd made it clear that wasn't happening. Just friends. She hated that expression.

But she was glad to have Hunter as her friend. And Gracie. Sweet, amazing Gracie. As much as Raven loved her family, it was good to have a few good friends, too. And they were good friends—even if she hadn't told them about her returning memories.

A few more bits and pieces had come back to her. She could see the man—the monster—but he didn't have a face. She could feel him kicking her and yelling at her. It was frustrating and a little bit scary.

Actually more than a little bit.

When she hadn't had any memories, it hadn't been real.

Now it was.

And Raven was second guessing all her decisions. Especially the book deal—which was moving faster than she'd expected. Julie had kept her promise and found a publisher who'd agreed to Raven's anonymity. And they were doing a rush job to get the book ready for release. She'd received a much larger advance than she'd expected as a new author. Julie explained it was the intrigue of her story along with the mystery of what happened to her.

Raven supposed she could back out, but she really felt God wanted her to write this book to help other people. And she could use the money. Now that she was out of rehab, the newspaper had officially released her from employment. She was still receiving a small amount of money from the disability insurance the paper had on all their reporters, but it would only last a few more months. Her new source of income would have to support her.

It was time to step back into the world. Even if she

wasn't sure if she wanted to be part of the news media anymore. But she had sent Marnie the article about Julie, her literary agent. Marnie had published it in their entertainment section and paid Raven as a freelance reporter.

As far as Raven was concerned that was the last newspaper article she planned to write. Once the book was published, she'd need to find a way to make a living.

She wandered out to the kitchen and grabbed a few cookies courtesy of Lydia. What an amazing baker the woman was. She should open a bakery. Raven stared at the cookie. A bakery?

Raven liked the idea of making other people happy by giving them tasty things to eat. She and Lydia could open the bakery together—if Lydia wanted. If not, Lydia could teach her how to bake and then she'd open it. She grinned as she chewed the last of the cookie. It really did sound like a great idea. She'd talk to Lydia about it tomorrow.

Raven wandered back out to the living room and settled in to watch the debates. The moderator was introducing the candidates: Marcia Ferris, Tomas Mendez, Hank Snow, and Charles Whitman, III. After introducing them, he asked each candidate why they wanted to be President.

Marcia Ferris: "I'm sure you're expecting me to say because I want to be the first female President, but the truth has nothing to do with my gender. I want to be President because I think I can help this country get back to core values and in so doing make this country great again."

Tomas Mendez and Hank Snow gave similar ideas.

She rolled her eyes. Blah...blah...blah. They all sounded the same.

Then it was Charles Whitman, III's turn. "I have one reason and one reason only why I want to be President. I love this country. I'm a patriot."

A patriot. Her pulse jumped as she stared at the screen. Everything turned wavy. He was walking toward her. Staring down at her, a look of disgust on his face. And he had something in his hand. A long stick. It came toward her. Pain shot through her body. Again and again and again. Her body shook as she trembled. She couldn't breathe. She gasped trying to get more air.

Raven screamed. She didn't want to remember anymore.

But with each electrical shot—another memory returned. And another. Eating and drinking out of dog bowls. Sleeping on straw. Being kicked. Being zapped with the electrical cattle prod. Raven lay on the sofa in a fetal position, trying to protect herself from the monster. Sweating. She touched the couch. The couch was real. The memories were not.

Not real. I'm not there. It's over. Not real. I'm safe. God is real. God loves me. She repeated these truths over and over.

Finally, she found the courage to open her eyes. She was in her house in Charm, Ohio. Not in some barn with the monster. Raven stared at the TV screen. She wasn't looking at what was really there. Instead, she was seeing Charles Whitman, III.

The monster had a face.

And a name.

20

"Charles Whitman, III."

Gracie stared at her. "You really think the frontrunner in the presidential race abducted you and held you prisoner?"

Raven had gone to see Gracie without an appointment. She hadn't slept at all last night. She'd been too afraid to close her eyes. "Of course not. I'm just telling you what I'm remembering. I know it's crazy. I know it's wrong. But it's what I remember."

"Good. I'm glad you know that."

"But why am I remembering him? I can't get his face out of my mind now."

"There's a very simple explanation for what's going on. Our mind fills in the unknown with the known. For example when you're talking with someone and watching TV at the same time, you may only hear part of both things but your mind fills in the unknown with the known. It works fine until someone veers off the path and says something that doesn't make sense."

"But why him?"

"You already told me that you've had several breakthroughs with your memories. But you couldn't remember the face. You were probably thinking about that and so when you saw his, your mind made the connection to him."

"Why not any of the other candidates' faces they were showing?"

"I don't know. I'm sure you've heard the saying the heart wants what the heart wants but let me tell you—the brain does what the brain wants to do. As much as we'd like to be able to explain everything that happens in our brains—we can't. And we can't always believe what our mind tells us. It's not infallible."

"So you don't think I'm losing it?"

"Not at all. I'd be more worried if you really believed that Charles Whitman actually had something to do with your abduction but you don't think that. Right?"

Raven knew the right answer but was it the truth? "Right. It would be ridiculous to think that Charles Whitman abducted me."

"So you're good. Probably tired, since you didn't sleep last night, but good."

"What about the fact I passed out?"

"Yeah, that's not good. I'm pretty sure it was brought on by the intensity and anxiety of remembering. Lots of people feel faint when they have anxiety attacks. They don't usually actually faint. But you've been through a lot of trauma, Raven. The intensity of the memories are probably what made you faint."

"I think it may have been better when I didn't remember."

"You know what they say about being careful what you pray for." Gracie smiled. "But God must think you're strong enough to handle it now. But if you faint again, I think you should see a neurologist just to make sure nothing's wrong."

"My Amish neighbor thinks it's connected to my blood sugar levels."

"Smart lady. That's possible too. Maybe you should have a full medical work-up. Agreed?"

"I guess. When my new insurance kicks in." She took a deep breath, glad she'd confided in Gracie. "On a happier note, I have an idea."

"About what?"

"About what to do in the next phase of my life."

"Really? That's good to be thinking about your future. What's the idea?"

"To open a bakery."

Gracie looked at her for a moment. "I thought you told me you weren't a good cook."

"I'm not, but my Amish neighbor is an amazing baker. I'm hoping she wants to become my partner or my teacher."

Gracie laughed as she shook her head. "OK, I'll be your guinea pig as you learn how to bake."

"Do you think the bakery is a good idea?"

"It could be. If you find out you like to bake. Especially since you're in a tourist area."

Raven stood. "I'd better go so you can get on with your regularly scheduled day. I'm sorry I interrupted it, but I was so freaked out. Thanks so much for seeing me."

"No problem. I hope you feel better."

"Much." Raven leaned down and hugged her. "You're a good friend."

When she got home, she went directly to Lydia's.

"I have an idea, Lydia. I think we should open a bakery together."

Lydia stared. "A bakery. Us?"

"Why not? You're an amazing baker. You could bake and I could run the business part. But I'd like you to teach me to bake too."

"My goodness. I chust never thought of me working. But the truth is I do get bored, sitting here with nothing to do. It was different when I was on the farm. There was always things that needed done. A bakery, you say?"

"A bakery. Hopefully right here in town."

"My goodness. It sounds like a good idea but I'll have to pray about it for a while and see what God says."

"Sounds like a plan."

Back in her own house, Raven couldn't get the name out of her head. Charles Whitman, III. She'd assured Gracie that she knew it wasn't him, but how could she be so certain? She couldn't remember the face of the monster. What did she remember about him from her research? She searched her memory banks but it came up blank. She walked to the spare bedroom she'd turned into an office/workout room.

She should let it go. Not give any credence to such a ridiculous idea. But it wouldn't hurt to check him out. She turned on the computer. As she skimmed articles, her heart skidded to a stop.

She couldn't breathe and everything turned wavy. No. I won't pass out. Keep me in the moment, God. She forced herself to take a deep breath and then another and another. When the dizziness passed, she looked back at the computer screen. Charles Whitman, III was from a small town in West Virginia. Great Cacapon. The same name as the river she'd been found in.

Coincidence?

21

Raven walked into the motel room in Berkeley Springs, West Virginia, the closest town to Great Cacapon that had motels. How would she explain this to Gracie? Or to anyone? One minute she was looking at her computer screen and the next she'd packed a bag and driven here. The whole drive she kept telling herself to turn around, to go back home. She kept driving.

And now here she was. In Morgan County, West Virginia. The place they'd found her broken body. And the home of Charles Whitman, III.

It wasn't rational.

As much as she didn't want to, she had to make a few phone calls so no one would be worried about her when they realized she wasn't at her house. Hunter was supposed to stop in after his shift.

If she told them where she was and why, they'd overreact. Especially Gracie. Just the fact that she was twenty miles from Charles Whitman's family home might make Gracie think that Raven had lost touch with reality. And she hadn't.

Or had she?

It was a little bizarre to just jump in her car and drive for seven hours. What was she planning on doing? Go to his house and ask him if he'd abducted her? Raven believed Gracie's explanation of the mind filling in the unknown with the known, but a smidgeon of doubt held sway.

In the motel room, Raven called her sister, hoping it went to voice mail. It didn't. "Hey Amanda."

"Where are you, Raven? I stopped by your house and you weren't there. Did you forget I was coming today?"

"Uh…I guess I did. Sorry. I'm uh…I took a road trip. Just needed to get away for a few days."

"Why?" Her sister demanded. "Is something wrong? And where are you?"

She picked one question to answer. "There's nothing wrong. I just needed to get away. It's not like I have a job or anything to prevent me from taking a little trip."

"I guess that's true but why didn't you tell me?"

"It was spur of the moment. I didn't really plan it. It just sort of happened." That was certainly true. "I was feeling a bit stressed out, so I took a short trip."

"Why are you stressed out?"

Amanda would want to know every little detail and Raven didn't want her to know the horrible things she'd experienced. "Maybe I've been doing too much lately. So, I thought a few days away would be good."

There was a long pause, but finally Amanda asked, "Where did you go?"

"Oh, just a cute little town in West Virginia."

"Where?" Her sister's voice had gone from compassionate to suspicious. Amanda knew her too well. "Please tell me you aren't down in the area where they found you. What was it called again?"

"Great Cacapon."

"Is that where you are?"

"I just wanted to see it for myself. To see the area—the river. To see if it jogged my memory."

"Oh, Raven. I don't like that you're down there alone. If you wanted to go, you should have asked me to come with you."

At least Amanda hadn't said it was a stupid idea. And Amanda was right, she shouldn't have come alone. But it was too late now. She was here. And she was all alone.

22

As Raven walked from her motel to the Sheriff's Department, she realized just how alone she was—and vulnerable. Any one of the people she passed could be the monster that had held her captive for months and then dumped her body in the Cacapon River.

What if he saw her and followed her? And the scariest part was he could walk right up to her and she wouldn't even know it was him. Because her mind had painted the picture of a presidential candidate as the monster.

Clearly that was impossible. But someone somewhere had hurt her. Tried to kill her. And probably still wanted her dead. Who was the monster? And where was he?

The blue sky turned wavy. She couldn't find her next breath. Her body shook. Looking down at the sidewalk, it looked more like a river. Take a breath, Raven. A deep breath. She did but everything still kept moving. She fell against a nearby building. Another deep breath.

"Are you all right?

She startled at the sound of a voice and opened her eyes.

A man, probably in his forties, stood there.

"Just a little dizzy."

It could be him. Her pulse zoomed, and she couldn't breathe. Calm down. He's not the monster. Not the monster. She forced a deep breath. God is with me. God is with me. The world came back into focus.

"Should I call 911?"

She shook her head. "I'm better now. Guess I should have eaten lunch."

He looked doubtful. "Are you sure?"

She forced a smile. "Right as rain. I'll be fine, but thanks for stopping to check on me."

He smiled. "OK, then. I'll be on my way."

After he walked away, Raven wanted to plop down on the sidewalk, curl up in a ball, and cry. Her knees were so wobbly she wasn't sure if they would hold her up. She needed to rest for a few minutes. But that would only cause another scene, so she resumed walking. One step at a time.

The Sheriff Department was housed in a brick building at the end of the block. When she got there, she took a few deep breaths. A small sign beside the door had the official seal on it.

She walked in, immediately appreciating the cool air. No one was at the counter. She dinged the bell sitting on the counter.

A few seconds later, a woman appeared. "I'm so sorry. I was in the back eating a little snack. I didn't hear you come in. Can I help you?"

"I was hoping to talk to Sheriff Matthew Borden. Does he still work here?"

"He sure does, but he's out on patrol right now. What's this about?"

What indeed? "I...uh...I'm Raven Marks. A while back—"

"I know exactly who you are, sweetheart. You seem to be doing much better than when you were here. Praise the Lord. You've been in my prayers for many months."

Had she met this woman? If so, she couldn't remember. "Did we meet?"

"Not at all. But I know about you. Our whole church has been praying for you"

That should have been comforting but wasn't. The thought that so many strangers knew who she was…was sort of scary. Raven forced a smile. "The prayers worked. I'm getting stronger every day."

"Praise the Lord."

"Amen to that." Raven liked this woman. "I just sort of came down here on a whim, but I was hoping to thank Sheriff Borden and maybe have him take me to where I was found."

"Still can't remember anything, huh?"

She didn't want to lie to this sweet woman. "Not really. Nothing concrete. I was hoping if I saw the area, it might help. Anything to catch the monster."

"I can't even imagine what you've been through or what it's like to not remember. Hold on. Let me get him back here. Won't take but a minute." She pointed at some chairs. "Feel free to sit down and relax."

Raven walked over to a chair and sat. Between the two chairs was a small table with a few out of date magazines. She picked one up. The world turned wavy—it had a huge picture of Charles Whitman, III on the cover.

God is with me. God is with me. The world came back into focus. This had to stop. Developing these anxiety issues was horrible. Would getting all her memories back make the anxiety go away? Or make them worse?

The woman walked from behind the counter and sat down in the other chair. "He'll be here in a minute. My name's Martha, by the way. I'm the evening dispatcher and receptionist all rolled up in one."

"Nice to meet you, Martha."

She touched the magazine. "He's our most famous citizen, you know. Everyone around here is so proud of him. It's amazing to think little Chuckie Whitman could become the next President of the United States."

Raven didn't want to talk about little Chuckie. "So do you know him?"

"Oh, sure. We graduated together. Even went to a hayride together." Martha looked past her, obviously remembering. "Once."

"Why not again?"

"We…we…" Her voice faltered. Again, she stared past Raven. Then she shook her head. "We just weren't a good match. Besides I met my future husband on the hayride. One look and I knew he was the man for me. Forever. Actually a boy at the time, but I still knew he was the one." She held up her left hand. "Twenty-four years and counting."

"That's wonderful."

"Martha, are you boring her with your life story?"

"And here's my handsome husband."

Raven smiled. "Good thing I didn't say anything bad about the sheriff, huh?"

"It wouldn't have bothered me none, sweetheart. He's a good husband but can be a bit brusque when he's wearing that old hat of his."

"Don't start with me, Martha."

The two shared a glance filled with love and trust. How wonderful to share a life. It had never been a goal to find her one true love but watching these two she realized that she might be missing something because of that decision.

Matthew turned to her. "It's so good to see you up and moving, Miss Marks. It's nothing short of miraculous."

"God is good."

Martha patted her hand. "Oh, yes He is, sweetheart. It was so nice to meet you. Now I'll leave the two of you alone." She stood and walked away.

Matthew took a seat beside her. "I'm sorry I don't have any good news to report on your case. I wish there was, but there's not. So what brings you here today, Miss Marks?"

"Please, call me Raven. I want to see the spot where you found me. Is that possible?"

"More than possible, but why?"

"I was hoping it might jog my memory. To help with the investigation."

"So you still don't remember anything?"

"Nothing important." Like a face. The right face and not the one in her imagination.

"Not remembering might be a blessing."

"You might be right, but...I just need to know that I've done everything I can to try to remember. It... it just seems important. What if...what if he's kidnapped someone else and I didn't do everything I could to stop him? To find him?"

"I pray you're wrong about that. Of course, I'll be glad to take you. You want to go right now? Probably be better to wait until tomorrow. When there's more light. It'll be dark soon."

She shuddered inwardly, not even wanting to think about being there in the dark. "Tomorrow will be fine."

"OK, then. Where are you staying?"

"The Inn."

"Great. I'll pick you up at nine."

23

Raven stared down into the ravine. Trees and bushes. The bottom wasn't visible. Neither was the river. It was a miracle she'd been found. "How could anyone have seen me down there?"

"They couldn't from here. It was two kayakers in the river. They saw you and called for help. Got you out of the water and stayed with you until we got there. Then it was pretty tricky getting you up here so we could get you to the hospital."

"How did you?"

"Actually, we ended up putting you on a boat and taking you to a waiting helicopter that flew you directly to Cumberland."

"Do you think I was thrown from here?"

"I don't think so. If this were the spot, you would have just ended up somewhere in the brush between here and the bottom. Chances are you wouldn't have made it to the river, and you were in the river. Not sure how long you were in the water, but you had hypothermia."

"I want to go down there." Actually she needed to see the spot. The place where she'd almost died. But God had intervened. It was just as Dr. Schaeffer said. It wasn't her time. God had a reason to save her. Maybe someone else needed saving from the monster?

"You can't get there from here. But there's a trail that will get you down to the river and then we can backtrack to the spot. It'll take a few hours to get there and back. But if you think you're up to it, we can do it."

"Oh, I can't ask you to spend that much time with me. You've already spent more than you should have. I can't take you away from your duties like that."

"I'm the sheriff. I pretty much work twenty-four hours a day when needed. So it's not a problem. Besides hiking is one of the things I do for fun, so I'll get a good workout as well." He patted his stomach. "Gotta keep looking handsome for Martha, you know."

"Are you sure?"

"Let me see your shoes."

She held up a foot.

"OK. Those are good sturdy shoes."

She'd given up fashion shoes since having to learn to walk again. She just didn't have it in her to wobble around on heels anymore. Comfort won over fashion these days.

"Let me call Martha to let her know we're going. I've got a backpack in of the trunk. It has water and energy bars. Plus a first-aid kit." He was already walking back to his cruiser.

"It sounds like you knew what we'd be doing today."

He smiled. "I had an idea that you might want to. Are you sure you're up for it?"

"I can handle it." She was suddenly thankful that she'd been working out with Hunter.

The sheriff drove a few miles down the road to

another spot. "OK, this is it. It's not too bad of a trail. Just be careful and move at your own speed. There's no rush."

An hour later Raven plopped down on a huge rock. "Oh, my goodness. I'm exhausted. And that was going downhill."

"But you made it. Considering less than a year ago, you couldn't walk, I'd say that's pretty awesome." He handed her a water bottle and an energy bar.

"And you say you do this for fun?"

He chuckled. "Yeah, Martha won't come with me either. Thinks I'm crazy, but I love the challenge. Plus in my line of work, I never know what I might have to do on any given day." He pointed at the river. "We need to go about a mile back upriver. But it's easy compared to what you just did. There's only one problem."

"Getting back up?"

He nodded. "Smart girl—oops, I mean smart woman. If you want, I can get one of my deputies to pick us up in his boat. That won't be a problem at all. He loves it when he gets to use the boat."

She shook her head. "No, I want to try to do this. Now that I'm here I don't feel like giving up."

"Knowing your limits is not giving up, Raven. It's smart."

She smiled. "That's good to know. I'll think about it." She stood up.

They started walking. He was right. It was much easier since they were on flat ground. The river rippled, some places it was smooth and other places it was white from the rocks in the river.

Finally, the sheriff stopped walking. "This is the spot."

"How can you tell?"

He pointed at the river. "Those three rocks. We call them The Triplets. You were wedged in them. The current took you to them. It's probably what saved your life."

A chill went up her spine. Her pulse was racing, and she fought against hyperventilating. God is with me. God is with me. Everything turned wavy. God is with me. She forced a deep breath. And another. The world came back into focus.

"Are you OK, Raven?"

She nodded, not trusting herself to speak. Instead she walked to the water's edge and then looked up. Matthew was right. This couldn't have been the spot she'd been tossed from. She wouldn't have landed in the water.

Matthew stood back but kept a watchful eye on her.

She walked along the bank, trying to remember anything. Finally, she walked back to the sheriff. "Nothing looks familiar. I guess this was a waste of time."

"Not for me. It was a good hike, and at least you know you tried your best."

"I guess."

"So you want me to call my deputy for a ride in his boat?"

"No, I'm feeling pretty good. I think I can make it back." She looked up the river. "So when you put me on a boat, where did you take me? Upriver or downriver?"

"Downriver to a small town called Paw Paw. And then you were life-flighted to Cumberland."

She pointed upriver. "What's up that way?"

"More of this. Lots of woods. You're in the Cacapon National Forest."

"So nobody lives around here?"

"Oh, sure but not in the forest itself."

She wanted to ask where Charles Whitman lived. But that would only feed her delusion, so she kept the question to herself. "How do you think I got here?"

"I see what you're thinking. That maybe one of the people living near here might be the person who kidnapped you. I can see why you'd think that, but..." He shook his head. "The river was running fast then. We'd had a lot of rain. Anyone could have put you in the river from anywhere above this spot. I know all the people in this area. It wasn't any of them."

"How can you be sure?"

"I'm sorry I can't find the person who did this, but it could have been anyone. From anywhere."

It could have been anyone. And she could walk right up to the man and never know he was the monster. She looked over at the sheriff. And just like that Charles Whitman's face disappeared and was replaced by the man who stood there looking at her. It was him. The monster. The world crumbled. She couldn't breathe. She was with the monster. This time he would kill her. And there was nothing she could do about it. She'd asked him to bring her here.

"Are you OK, Raven?"

She couldn't speak. Couldn't move. She felt herself falling and the world disappeared.

~*~

Couldn't move her hands or her feet. The monster. She was back with the monster. The light purr of the motor. Back in the golf cart. Soon, he'd kill her. And this time he wouldn't fail. How had she let this happen? Again. She wouldn't survive this time, but she'd soon be home with God. It's OK. I'm ready, Father. Peace descended. She took a deep breath.

"I think she's awake," a voice said.

"It's OK, Raven. You're safe. You just passed out. You're in the boat. It's taking us back to Berkeley Springs."

She opened her eyes.

Matthew Borden stared down at her with concern and kindness.

Someone touched her cheek. "You're fine now, dear, but you gave us quite a scare," Martha said.

Matthew couldn't be the monster. Monsters didn't have sweet wives like Martha. Or did they? "What happened?"

"One minute you were fine, and then you started hyperventilating, and then you passed out. I called for a boat to pick us up. Martha came along. She was too worried to stay home."

Raven looked down. Her hands and feet were clamped in. "Why am I chained up?"

"Not chains, sweetie. Restraints. We couldn't have you waking up and jumping out of the boat. Or tipping us over. It was for your safety." Martha began to undo the clamps. "See I'm taking them off now. Nothing to worry about."

After the restraints were off, Raven moved to a sitting position. "I'm so sorry."

"Nothing to be sorry about." Matthew said with a smile. "I'm just glad you're all right. You gave me quite a scare."

Raven looked around as they glided down the river, surrounded by trees. The place seemed so peaceful. So beautiful. And yet some monster had tried to kill her by throwing her in this water. She brushed the thoughts away. Focus on the present. "So this is how you rescued me last time?"

"Pretty much. Except we're not going to Paw Paw but back toward Berkeley Springs."

"It's beautiful here." She was surrounded by God's beauty. She breathed in His holy Presence. Peace.

"It surely is." Martha agreed. "There's a lot of beauty in this world, Raven. Sometimes we have to make a choice whether to focus on the beauty or the evil."

Raven stared at Martha. She'd been focusing on the evil, trying to find out who'd hurt her. But at the same time, she was ignoring the beauty, the love, the goodness that was all around her.

God saved her that night for a reason. The monster intended for her to die. But she hadn't. She'd survived. God healed her broken body and was in the process of healing her broken spirit.

Would she waste her second chance by obsessing over a past she couldn't change? Or move forward into her future? God loved her no matter what the monster had done, and He had good plans for her. Maybe it was time for her to put the past in the past.

24

"I'm fine, Martha. Really."

They were back in Raven's motel room.

Martha sighed, clearly exasperated. "I just hate the thought of leaving you alone in this room after what happened. It just doesn't seem right. You're more than welcome to spend the night at our house. We won't even be around to bother you. My shift starts in a few hours."

"That's not necessary, but you are so sweet to offer. I promise I will call you or 911 if I start to feel dizzy again."

She gave her a stern look. "You promise?"

Raven put a hand over her heart. "I solemnly promise."

Martha laughed. "Well, I suppose that will have to do. But I will call you later to check on you. All right?"

"Sure." Raven gave her the phone number. "I really appreciate all you've done. And Matthew too. You've both gone way beyond the call of duty."

Martha blushed. "Well, thanks for that. I'll talk to you in a few hours."

Raven held up her phone. "I'll keep it close by."

After Martha left, Raven laid down on the bed, exhausted, physically and mentally. She couldn't keep passing out like that. She needed to get the anxiety under control. It really had been better before she'd started remembering. She wished she could go back to not knowing.

Not knowing about the barn. The cattle prod. The monster. But she did know—at least parts of it. But it was what she didn't know that terrified her.

The identity of the monster.

She wanted to let go of the past and move forward, but one recurring thought kept her from doing that. What if he'd kidnapped someone else? What if there was another woman in those chains right this moment?

She opened the nightstand beside the bed. Just what she was looking for. A Bible. She turned to the concordance and looked under anxiety, then turned to John 14.

Peace I leave with you; my peace I give you. I do not give to you as the world gives. Do not let your hearts be troubled and do not be afraid.

But she was troubled and afraid. So very afraid. "Please, God. I want Your peace. I'm tired of being afraid of everything and everybody." Especially the monster.

Who was the monster? First she'd seen the face of Charles Whitman, and then Matthew Borden. Obviously she couldn't trust her own memories. It was ridiculous to think either of them had anything to do with her abduction.

But why had she fixated on these men? She understood Matthew. He'd been standing in front her. But what about Charles Whitman? And what about the coincidence that he was from this area where they'd found her broken body?

"I know it must be a delusion, but I can't stop thinking about him." No matter how crazy it was, she needed to see Charles Whitman's house. To see if he had a barn. Her barn. But what if it was? What would she do then? How would she get anyone to believe her?

"One step at a time." She grabbed her keys and her purse. She was almost out the door when she realized she'd forgotten her phone. That wouldn't have been good. The last thing she wanted to do was to worry Martha.

After getting her phone, she walked to the counter in the lobby.

A young man rushed over. "Are you leaving us so soon?"

"Actually, no, I'm not leaving until tomorrow morning. I have a strange request."

"Probably not as strange as some of the requests I've had. You can't even imagine what it's like working in a hotel."

She laughed. "You're probably right about that. I came down here for one reason, but I found out that Charles Whitman lives in the area. Is that right?"

"He sure does."

"I'd love to see his house. Do you know where he lives?"

"Everyone around here knows where he lives. You drive over the mountain to Great Cacapon. Now don't blink, or you'll miss it. It's not much to look at. Then you drive about two miles past Great Cacapon and you'll see a big white house on the left. You can't miss it."

"A white house. I guess he likes living in them."

"Isn't that the truth? I think he'll make it to the

other White House. At least I hope he does. He'll make a great President." He laughed. "Anyway it's got a long drive, and you aren't allowed to go back there, but you can see the house from the road."

"Oh, great. I'll take a few pictures to show all my friends."

"While you're here, make sure you go see our castle too."

"Castle?"

"Yep, it's a real castle. It was built by some man for his wife. I guess you could say he treated her like a queen."

"I guess you could say that. Thanks, I might just do that."

Raven clutched the steering wheel as she drove up the mountain, glad she didn't have to drive this road every day. Especially in the winter. It would be treacherous when it snowed.

She came to the tiny town of Great Cacapon. The clerk was right—not much there. She kept driving. She looked down at the mileage so she could keep track. Almost exactly two miles later she saw the huge white house on the left.

She slowed but didn't stop.

She turned around at the next drive and drove past the house again. Even slower this time. Nothing looked familiar. No alarms went off in her head. Not a shred of anxiety. And it wasn't even on the river side of the mountain.

Once again, she turned around.

As she approached the house for the third time, she suddenly made a decision and turned in. No one stopped her. She drove up the lane. Still no one stopped her. Her gaze took in the property.

The house was large but not quite a mansion. It was in the elegant style of a pre-Civil War home with pillars and a portico. Off to the side was what looked to be a garage but still matched the style of the house—even had pillars.

Behind the house a barn—a huge barn.

Her pulse raced.

Charles Whitman, III did have a barn.

The world turned wavy. Very deliberately Raven slowed her breathing. This was not the place or time to have another anxiety attack. As she was deep breathing a man walked around the corner of the house. He motioned at her.

She rolled down her window.

"This is private property, ma'am. You can't be here."

"I'm sorry. I needed to turn around, and I hated the thought of backing out on that crazy road."

"Not a problem. Are you lost? Can I help you in some way?"

"No. Not really. I just needed to turn around. This is a lovely house. Is it yours?"

"I'm the caretaker."

"Oh, I see. Does that mean you farm it?"

"We're a horse farm, ma'am."

"What kind of horses?"

"Thoroughbreds, of course. The owner loves his horses as you can tell by his barn. It's got all the bells and whistles. A workout arena and even a modern, glistening medical center for the horses. He doesn't spare expenses when it comes to his horses."

It didn't sound like the rickety old barn of her memories.

"Sounds beautiful. I don't suppose I could see it."

He shrugged. "I shouldn't really do that, but the boss is away so I don't see any harm in it. Come along."

She almost panicked. She hadn't really expected him to agree. Could this man be the monster? And luring her back to the barn? She took a deep breath. Please God, don't let me have an anxiety attack right now. She had to see the barn then she could put her delusion to rest.

She opened the car door. The man chatted amiably as he showed her around the barn and the arena. There were at least two other people working there that she saw.

She smiled at her tour guide. "It's a beautiful barn. Any other barns on the property? I have a thing about barns, especially old barns. I love the history behind them."

"Nope this is the only one. He had to tear down the old one to have this built."

"That's too bad. I'm sure it was a great barn."

They walked back to her car. She thanked the caretaker and drove down the lane, knowing this wasn't the place she'd been held captive.

25

Raven spent most of the drive home telling herself that this bizarre obsession that Charles Whitman had been involved in her disappearance was finished. She'd seen his house and even his barn. There were at least three people who worked there on a regular basis according to the caretaker.

No way, the senator could have kept her captive and those men not known about it. Plus, the barn wasn't a rickety old thing at all, but modern and elaborate. It was not her prison.

It was time to let go, but what if…what if her kidnapper had another woman? How could she let go of that? Weren't all women her neighbors? So, OK, she could agree that Charles Whitman, III wasn't her kidnapper.

But someone was.

And that someone could hurt other women. How could she just forget that? And yet, there was nothing she could do at this point. Raven shook her head. What was the right thing to do?

God had good plans for her. She needed to cooperate with God by letting go of the past and move forward. She had friends. Of course, she might wish one of them was more than a friend, but Hunter had made it clear that wasn't what he wanted. Still, friends were good. She was closer to Amanda than she'd ever been. And her two little nieces were the light of her life.

And there might be a bakery in her future. She daydreamed about that bakery. It really did seem like a good fit for her. And for Lydia.

Her life was moving forward. It was time to stop looking in the rearview mirror of her life. If she ever remembered the monster's face, then she could do something to stop him.

When she got back home to Charm, Raven found a box on her porch. She grinned as she lugged the box in the house. A few moments later, she pulled out a book.

Unsinkable by Jane Doe.

Happy tears rolled down her cheeks. She was thrilled. It didn't have her name on it, but Raven knew it was her book and that was enough. She'd be the only one to know. Not Hunter or Gracie. Not even her sister. God had wanted her to do this, but she didn't like baring her soul to anyone.

They would be so happy for her if they knew. But if they knew, they would read the book. And if they read the book, they'd know her most secret thoughts. She didn't mind sharing her secret thoughts with strangers but with family? Friends? It seemed too personal.

What was it Gracie had said last week during their session? Something about if one kept secrets from those around them, it meant that they either didn't feel what they were doing was the right thing, or one didn't trust them.

But that wasn't true.

Raven was sure the book had been the right thing to do. It had been therapy for her. And she certainly trusted her family and her friends. Then why was she keeping the book a secret? She sighed and brushed the thought aside.

This was all moving way faster than the norm in the publishing world. But everything was becoming instantaneous thanks to technology, even the notoriously slow publishing world. What used to take many months could be done in weeks these days.

After lugging the books to the bedroom, in case Amanda or anyone else showed up, she pulled out her phone and called her agent.

"I got the books."

"Great. I received a few copies as well. They look great. In fact, I just got off the phone with the PR department at the publisher. They're setting up several interviews for you next week on release day. In New York. The big time."

Her stomach twisted. This was really happening. "But they're sure they can keep me anonymous?"

"You have my word. In fact, I'm going with you to make sure everything goes smoothly. Plus, I have a plan. Now I have a few questions."

"OK."

"Would you like to be a blonde, a brunette? Maybe a redhead?"

Raven understood the plan. "You'll disguise me."

"It couldn't hurt, right?"

"Right. Red."

"Subtle or outlandish."

Raven smiled. "Outlandish."

"Excellent. Long? Short? Straight? Or curly?"

"Medium curly. And I'll bring some glasses."

"Really big glasses. And maybe practice an accent. Even though we'll disguise your voice, it helps even more."

"I'm great at accents. It's why I always got cast in plays in high school and college. What kind of an accent?" By the time she hung up, Raven was feeling more confident about the whole thing. She'd do these interviews and then come back to her simple life in Charm, Ohio.

Her phone rang again. "Hi, Hunter."

"Just seeing if you're back yet."

"Got back a little while ago. How'd you know I was gone?"

"Amanda told me at our session yesterday. Did you have a good time?"

"I guess that's one way of describing it." She felt horrible not telling him the real reason behind her trip.

"Want to go out and eat somewhere tonight? My shift just finished so I can be there in about thirty minutes."

"Sounds good."

As she changed her clothes, she stared at the boxes that felt like secrets. And that wasn't how she wanted to live her life. On the other hand, she wanted to get her message out there and then fade into the background. She had no desire to be a celebrity—not even a local one. She turned her back to the box. I'll just not think about it. Raven walked out to the kitchen and stared at the refrigerator. She really didn't want to go out to eat but she was too exhausted to cook. So she did the next best thing.

Her doorbell rang a few minutes later.

Hunter smiled as she opened the door.

It was good to see a friend—someone she could trust. Someone she knew wasn't the monster. "Come on in. I...uh...I hope you don't mind but I sort of changed the plans. I realized how tired I am."

"No dinner?"

"Dinner here."

"You're cooking?"

"Not exactly." She wrinkled her nose. "How do you feel about pizza?"

"Love it."

The doorbell rang again.

"And here it is."

He reached for his pocket.

"Don't even think about it, Hunter. My treat."

"But I asked you out for dinner."

"But—"

He walked past her and opened the door.

She caved and let him pay. A quick trip to the kitchen and she came back with cans of pop and a bag of chips piled up on the plates. "Oops, I forgot the napkins."

When they were settled in, she looked at Hunter. Maybe she wasn't ready for a relationship yet, but this felt good—right. Hunter seemed to be a good man, one she wanted to know better. And yet she couldn't share her secrets with him. Did that say something about him—or was it more about her?

"So where did you go? Amanda just said you went on a short road trip."

She could at least tell him that much. "I went to Berkeley Springs, West Virginia. It's near the area where they found me."

"So, did it help you remember anything?" He didn't seem to be shocked or think it strange.

"No. It was a wasted trip for the most part."

"What part wasn't wasted?"

"I sort of had an epiphany."

"Epiphanies are always a good thing. Want to share yours?" He quickly added. "But you don't have to if you're not ready. Epiphanies can be very personal."

"I don't mind. I realized that God has blessed me with a second chance. I should have died in that river, but I didn't. And instead of focusing on that, I've been obsessing over a past I can't remember. It's time for me to enjoy my present and to look toward the future."

He grinned. "Wow. That's a pretty good epiphany. Any chance I might be part of it?"

"Well, I did share my epiphany with you."

"Yes you did. You know I don't think I've ever had a conversation where the word epiphany was used as many times as we've used it tonight."

"And you just used it again." She laughed. "So I have another trip I have to take next week."

"My, my, you're becoming quite the traveler. Where are you going this time?"

She had a story prepared to tell, not just to him but to Amanda and Gracie as well. A story? More like a lie. "I…uh…I've been thinking about how to make a living and still live in Charm. So I'm checking into some possibilities." Not quite the truth but not quite a lie either.

"Sounds intriguing. I sure hope it works out. I'd like you to stay." He placed a hand over hers. Maybe he didn't want to be just friends?

"Me, too."

After Hunter left, Raven cleaned up, and then walked into her bedroom. The box sat in the middle of her floor. She should have told him about the book—and about the things she was remembering. And she would—soon.

26

"So what's with the Jane Doe name? You don't actually think anyone believes that's your real name, do you?" Shanley DeForest smiled.

From where Raven sat, it was as fake a smile as the woman's eyelashes. "Of course not, because it's not my real name."

"Could it be that you're not using your real name because none of your story is true? That you made all this up for your fifteen minutes of fame?" Shanley's tone bordered on hostile.

Raven forced a smile—not sure why since her face couldn't be seen by the viewers. "It's all very true. I wish it weren't, but it is."

"Then why not give us details so your readers and I can verify the facts. Like the name of the hospital or the river where you were found. How are we supposed to believe all this without knowing any facts?"

Raven pushed down her anger. This hadn't been part of the deal when she'd agreed to the interviews. "Because those aren't the details, I want people to focus on. I want them to focus on the power of God to get each of us through the storms we all face in this life. My story might not be the same as someone else's, but God promises never to forsake us, and He never does."

"God?" The woman practically rolled her eyes. "I'd think you'd be angry at God for letting this happen to you. If it happened at all."

Raven ignored the last part and focused on God. "God didn't want this to happen to me."

"Then why did it?"

"Because there's evil in this world. Someone made a choice to do evil. God gives each of us a choice. Some people make the right choice and others don't."

"God's supposed to be all-powerful. That means He could have stopped it, right?" Shanley's expression showed interest. "Why didn't He? Doesn't He love you?"

Raven's stomach knotted. She hadn't been prepared for this type of questioning. It wasn't that she minded, but she was messing it all up. "I'm sure He could have, but He gives all of us free will to choose good or evil. Most of us choose good, but there is real evil out there in the world."

"Since you believe so much in this God, why didn't He help you?"

"He did. I survived. Not just survived, I'm doing fantastic now. The doctors said I probably wouldn't walk again but I am. I'm slowly rebuilding my life. None of that would have or could have happened without God."

"Now where exactly did you say those doctors treated you at?" Fake smile once again.

"I didn't say. And I won't say."

"As a journalist, I find it hard to accept your story without some basic facts. It wouldn't be the first time a wannabe writer made up a horrific story just so they could get published."

"The publisher has a note in the book. They've

verified my injuries, my hospital stay, and my time at a rehabilitation center. None of it's made up."

"So why not tell the world the real story? Or should I say the whole story?"

Raven was ready for this question. "The truth is because I'm afraid. Whoever kept me captive for months is still out there. If he knew I survived, he might come looking for me."

The interviewer smiled. "Well, I guess I can't argue with that." She held up the book. "The book is *Unsinkable* by Jane Doe. Thanks for being my guest on A View of The World. I'm Shanley DeForest."

~*~

Hunter stared at the TV screen. The first time he'd met Raven, she'd refused to tell him her name, so he'd called her Jane Doe. It couldn't be, could it? The writer didn't sound like Raven. The woman speaking had a sweet, soft southern accent. Nothing like Raven's.

But the story—the story was Raven's.

Raven wouldn't have written a book and not told anybody. Or maybe she did tell someone. The people who were important to her. Like Amanda. It wasn't as though she had to tell him if she didn't want to, but he'd thought their friendship was growing.

And Raven had taken a mysterious trip somewhere. She hadn't told him where she was going. Only that she was looking into options for her future.

A future he'd hoped they might share.

He'd told her he only wanted to be friends, because that was what she needed right now. Whether she wanted to admit it or not, she was fragile emotionally. He refused to take advantage of that.

He hit reverse and watched the interview again. And still couldn't decide if it was Raven. But if she could write a book and not tell him, maybe she wasn't the right person for him after all. He was done with secrets. His former fiancé had certainly loved hers.

~*~

Shanley motioned for them to cut. After they did, her smile disappeared. "I hope that makes my boss happy." She walked away without another word to Raven—not even a good-bye.

Raven stood there wondering what she'd done to upset the woman so much.

"Great job." Julie was by her side.

"I'm not so sure about that. She was so hostile."

"She's never happy about anything. The other interviews will go smoother. I promise."

"I hope so. That was brutal."

"I know. That's my fault. I didn't realize she would ask those types of questions. Or be that combative. She has a reputation for not being the easiest person to deal with. I guess I should have warned you."

"I just wish I'd done a better job."

"You did fine. Really." Julie handed her a bag and whispered, "OK, go change your wig and clothes. I'll meet you at the coffee shop across the street."

They repeated the process after every interview— live and taped. All their precautions seemed a little silly to Raven, but she was the one who wanted to remain anonymous. And was grateful for all Julie's hard work to keep her that way.

Julie was only doing what she'd asked. And Julie was right—the other interviews went much more smoothly. No one doubted her story. No one seemed angry at her. But when it was over, Raven was more than ready to go back home to her quiet life.

On the flight back to Cleveland, Julie looked over at her. "So...what's going on in that mind of yours?"

Raven wished she knew the answer. "I'm really not sure. I guess I'm so exhausted at this point, it's hard to think."

"What about what you're feeling?"

"Are you my therapist now?"

Julie patted her hand. "No, but I hope I'm your friend. You can talk to me, Raven."

Raven smiled. "I hope so too, but I'm fine. Just tired."

"I'm thinking you should be working on your next book. A follow-up to this one."

"Really?"

"Sure, everyone who reads this book will want to know what happened to you. What's going on in your life. And of course, just like this book, you can weave in spiritual truths that you've learned from your experience."

"Maybe, but what I'd really like to do is try my hand at fiction."

"Fiction. I don't see you as a fiction kind of person."

"I love to read fiction. Always have. In fact, I daydream about made-up characters and their stories. Maybe I should take one of those daydreams and write it down."

"Sounds like a plan and...we could use your pen name. Jane Doe. You'd already have a platform of readers who would buy your book. I love it. And your readers will love that you're doing so well. You should get started the minute you get back home."

"I'm surprised to hear you say that."

"Why? I represent fiction writers as well as non-fiction."

"I know but lot of people turn up their noses about fiction. As if it's trivial because it's not a true story."

"I'm not one of those persons. Jesus made up stories to make a point. They're called parables."

"I guess that's true. I never thought of it like that."

"Pray about it and write what the Holy Spirit puts on your heart."

27

The man stared at the television screen. It was his habit to scroll through the news channels during his free time—which was precious little now that he was so busy. As he listened to the interview with a woman who'd survived a fall and a kidnapping that she couldn't remember, his blood went cold. It couldn't be her. There was no way she could have survived.

And as vague as her details were, she could have been anyone from anywhere, not necessarily his Suzie Q. And that sweet, southern accent. His Suzie Q didn't have that. It wasn't a fake accent. It was as if she'd talked that way her whole life.

It couldn't be her.

But was he willing to take that chance? He was about to fulfill all of his dreams. All he had to do was not make any mistakes. Was Suzie Q the blunder that would keep him from his destiny? Even if she had somehow survived, she'd told all of America that she couldn't remember anything about her abduction or her abductor. No one would believe her if she accused him. Besides she'd said she had no idea who the monster was—that was the name she'd called him. Probably just a coincidence.

Monster.

He smiled at the memory.

It had been a rush to have her hidden all those months. Being in control. Her very existence depended on him. So much better than he'd thought it would be. He hadn't minded the extra work. Maybe it was time to find another…guest.

But maybe not.

He looked back at the TV screen. Could that have really been Suzy Q? He smiled. If it was her, the scopolamine had done its job. The authorities would surely have come knocking on his door by now if she'd remembered him in spite of what she'd said on TV. If it was really her.

No, nothing to worry about. It couldn't be her. There was no way she could have survived. He walked over to his laptop and typed in Berkeley Springs Monitor and the date of August thirtieth. He remembered the date well. He'd scoured the paper every day until he saw what he was waiting for. He pulled up the Internet version and scanned. There it was.

Jane Doe Pulled from Cacapon River.

Today a group of kayakers came upon the body of an unknown victim of the river. According to the coroner, she'd been dead for more than thirty-six hours. They have no clues to her identity at this time.

The timeline fit perfectly with his Suzie Q. There was no reason to think it wasn't her. When he'd read it the first time, he'd been so sure it was Suzie Q that he hadn't bothered to follow up with the authorities.

But now he wasn't quite as sure.

How could he do that without alerting the authorities of his interest in the case? He continued scanning later editions of the paper. And there it was.

Jane Doe Identified.

He scrolled down the article. And then he saw it. Not the name he expected. Turned out that Jane Doe had been a lone hiker who'd apparently had an accident and tumbled in the river.

He pounded a fist on the desktop.

How had he missed that? Talk about a blunder. He should never had assumed the Jane Doe was Suzie Q. He couldn't afford those kind of blunders. He pounded on the desk again and again.

A knock. "It's time for your next appointment."

He flicked off the computer, stood up, and put on his mask. Then he turned to face his assistant. "Robert, I need you to change my schedule. I need a few days off."

Robert looked concerned. "Is there something wrong? Anything I can help with?"

Oh, he wished that were the case, but this was something he had to take care of himself. "Nothing's wrong. I just need some time to myself."

"I'm sure I can manage that. But you'll have to wait for a few days."

"Not a problem." He needed time to prepare. "And I need you to check on something for me, but it has to be kept in confidence."

"You can trust me, sir."

"I need you to find out about a reporter on the Marietta paper. I'm not sure if she still works there."

"Looking for a new PR person, huh?"

What a perfect front. "I'm considering it."

"Sounds like a good idea."

"Her name is Raven Marks.

28

Raven stepped out of her garage. She tugged the rollaway suitcase behind her.

"Raven, you are back. I'm so glad to see you. I chust couldn't wait until you came back so I could tell you about this bakery idea of yours." Lydia was beaming.

Raven repressed a sigh. This wasn't the right time. She was too tired—no, more like exhausted. Ten interviews in three days. It had been a crazy schedule but she and Julie both agreed that doing all of them as quick as possible lessened the chance of anyone finding out her real identity. Not wanting to hurt Lydia's feelings she forced a smile. "I'm back."

"I've been praying about it. I was taking a walk the other day and found the perfect location. It was a small restaurant, so it already has equipment in it. I called the owner and he's willing to lease the place to us. I believe it's a sign from God, yes?"

"Maybe."

"You've changed your mind? You don't want to open the bakery?" Lydia sounded disappointed. "Or maybe it's me. Maybe I'm not the right person for a partner. I can understand that. I don't know anything about running a business. You can still rent the building with a different partner. I won't be angry."

"No. No. It's not that at all. I do want to open the bakery with you. I'm just exhausted from my trip. That's all. Can we talk about this tomorrow?"

"Of course. Of course. I'm so sorry. It was rude of me not to see how tired you are. You go to sleep. We'll talk more tomorrow, yes."

"You're not rude; you're an angel, Lydia. And absolutely yes. Thank you." She made her way to her porch.

"Well, I'm not an angel, but you go rest now. Straight to bed with you." Lydia made shooing motions with her hands. "Good night."

"Good night." Without bothering to unpack, Raven curled up on the sofa. Sleep sneaked up on her and then the dreams came…

A man with no face walked toward her holding out a long stick that glowed green. Closer and closer.

"No. I don't want it. Go away."

He came closer. He had a faint green glow as well, but the green stick was even brighter. So bright it hurt her eyes.

"Take it."

"No."

"You have no choice. Take it." Now he glowed as bright as the stick. She couldn't tell where the stick ended, and the man started. He just kept moving toward her.

"I don't want it. Go away."

He was in front of her holding out the stick. "Take it. Now. It's belongs to you. Take it now."

Tears streamed down her cheeks. "I don't want it." But even as she said the words, her hand moved toward the green glow. She didn't want to touch the evil. But her hand kept moving toward it.

"You have no choice. Take it…take it…take it…"

So much pain. She didn't want it. She tried to let go but her fingers wouldn't release it. She was glowing. As bright as the stick. As bright as the monster. She looked at the monster. The monster had her face.

She was the monster.

Raven screamed and bolted upright. She stared around the room, jumping at the shadows, looking for…she didn't know what. Her heart hammered and sweat rolled down her back. The shadows morphed into her living room, dimly lit, but recognizable.

Only a dream. Not real. She wiped away the tears. Not real. But what if the dream was trying to tell her something?

Raven shuddered.

Her phone buzzed. She spoke out loud, calming her voice. "Hi, Gracie."

"Just checking to see if you're coming tomorrow."

Tomorrow. Her therapy Bible study. As much as she'd meant to get serious about reading the Bible, she hadn't had time that week. "Oh, I'm glad you called. I can't make it tomorrow. Something came up."

"OK. But these sessions are important."

"I know. I know. I'll make it up. We can do two next week."

Gracie laughed. "Whatever."

"Hey, Gracie, let me ask you a question."

"Sure."

"What do you think about dreams? Do you believe God speaks to us through our dreams?"

"I think there are all sorts of reasons we have specific dreams. And sometimes we just have dreams for no particular reason."

"That doesn't help much."

"Maybe we could discuss it further if we were having a session tomorrow."

"Yeah, yeah…I hear you. But, really? Do you think dreams…I'm not sure how to word it…but do you think God can uses dreams to give us messages?"

"Of course, but you have to be careful to not make more out of a dream than it really is. Sometimes dreams are just crazy manifestations of our subconscious. What was your dream?"

"Nothing really. I was just curious."

"There's the Raven I know and love. Always willing and ready to share her thoughts with her friends."

"Sarcasm is not a nice thing, Gracie."

"I suppose not. I'll put on my psychologist hat for just a moment. You've been through a lot of trauma and, in fact, you're still going through it as the memories come back. Each time you remember something new, it's as if you're experiencing it for the first time. So considering that, it would surprise me if you weren't having some nightmares."

"So nothing to worry about?"

"Exactly."

"Thanks for the mini session. I promise I won't miss next week."

"I'm holding you to that."

Raven hung up. Nothing to worry about. It was just a dream. But what if it wasn't? What if God was trying to tell her that her monster was out there? Looking for her. Coming for her.

She should never have written the book. What had she been thinking? If the monster read it or saw her on

TV, he would know she was still alive. And that would make him angry.

Why…oh, why had she written it? She'd been so sure it was something God wanted her to do but now? It seemed like one big mistake.

29

Why can't I be strong? I know God is with me but I...
Raven sat in a corner of her bedroom closet wiping away tears. It was the only place she felt safe. Intellectually, she knew it wasn't true. The truth was there was no real safety in the closet—or anywhere else. Not for her. As long as the monster was free, she was in danger. She'd told herself that she would let go of the past she couldn't remember and focus on the future—make her own memories in the present.

Instead, it chased her down in her dreams when she slept and visions when she was awake. It was an ever-present fear.

God must be so disappointed in her.

The thought brought on a fresh set of tears. Before all this, she thought she was a good Christian but if that were true then why couldn't she get past all of this? She'd believed the things she'd written. And yet here she sat in her closet — terrified.

Julie had assured her that people were being helped by the book. The reviews Raven had read online agreed with Julie. But now Raven was afraid it had been a mistake that could cost her life.

She'd been sure writing the book was what God wanted but now that it was out there, she regretted it.

All her life she'd watched as good Christian people went through a storm or a crisis, even lost loved ones. And though they'd grieved, they'd stayed in faith.

She'd thought she had that kind of faith but in the last few days, she'd fallen apart. And she couldn't seem to put herself back together. Instead, she sat in a closet while her mind played the bits and pieces of her captivity as if it were an old film. No sound, only the blinking black and white visions in the shadows. The monster walking toward her. Kicking her. Coming at her with that horrible cattle prod. Her sprawled out on a floor. And the pain. She could remember the pain in agonizing detail.

Sometimes the monster had Charles Whitman's face. But just as often it was Sheriff Matthew Borden's face. And sometimes no face.

She hadn't left the house since she'd returned from New York. She hadn't answered her phone or her door. The euphoria she'd felt in New York had turned to terror she had no control over.

She'd thought she was ready to look forward to the future. A bakery with Lydia. A friendship with Hunter—or maybe even more—until the nightmares started. And everything had gone downhill since then. Now she sat in her closet crying out to God, but He didn't seem to be listening to her.

I will never forsake you. You are the one not listening.

Raven stilled. Deep in her soul the truth resonated. Gracie had told her more than once that God would speak to her through His Holy Word. And she believed that, but it hadn't made her actually study His Word.

Raven crawled out of the closet to her nightstand. Picking up the Bible, index cards scattered to the floor. Gracie had given them to her with Bible verse references. Raven hadn't bother to look up the verses. She gathered them up and turned the pages until she found it.

2 Timothy 1:7. *For the Spirit God gave us does not make us timid, but gives us power, love and self-discipline.*

Sitting in a closet was definitely timid. She moved on to the second reference.

Proverbs 29: 25. *Fear of man will prove to be a snare, but whoever trusts in the Lord is kept safe.*

Her fear had trapped her—literally and figuratively. But this verse promised that God would keep her safe. Of course, that didn't mean something bad couldn't happen to her here on earth but even if it did, she would be with God. That night when the monster tossed her off the cliff, she hadn't felt fear. God's love had surrounded her as she hurtled through space, twinkling stars spinning in her vision, to what she thought would be her death. God kept her safe that night and he would continue to keep her safe. She'd forgotten that. The monster was stealing her life because she was allowing fear to control her.

These verses were amazing. How had Gracie known to choose these specific verses?

Raven knew the answer.

God.

She looked at the next card.

1 Peter 5: 7. *Cast all your anxiety on Him because He cares for you.*

That was exactly what she needed to do. Give God her anxiety. He'd protected her from the monster once before because He loved her. He could be trusted to do it again.

More tears streaked her cheeks, but these were different. *I'm so sorry, God. I've been more focused on evil than on Your love—Your power—Your goodness. I'm casting all my anxiety on You. Take it. I don't want it.*

Take it. That's what the monster had said in her dream. She'd taken the awful green glowing stick. A stick that represented evil, fear, and pain. But she was giving it to God. She sat on the floor wiping away her tears as the burden lifted.

The doorbell rang.

The fragile connection broke—paralyzing fear surfaced.

Raven fought it. *I will not fear—God is with me.* Her racing heart slowed. Peace descended. But she was in no shape to talk to anyone right now.

Footsteps sounded across the floor.

Someone was in her house. She looked around for something to protect herself. She needed to buy a gun. She couldn't move. She tried to remember Hunter's lessons, but her mind blanked.

"Raven. Are you here?"

Amanda.

Relief flooded so fast, Raven had to hold on to the door frame to stand up. She wiped away her tears. "Hold on, Amanda. I'll be out in a second." She rushed to the bathroom and washed her face, whispering, "I can do this. I can do this. God is with me. He did not give me a spirit of timidity but of love and power." She took a deep breath and walked out.

Amanda was sitting on the sofa. Her nieces sat beside her looking sweet with huge smiles. They both looked as if they'd bust.

"I'm sorry. Did I forget you were coming over?"

Her sister stared at her. "No you didn't. I've been calling and calling and you haven't been answering. Are you all right?"

"I'm fine. I'm sorry I didn't answer. I know that probably scared you. I won't do that again."

"Thanks."

"This is an unannounced visit," Her oldest niece said.

"Well, it's a wonderful surprise, Mallory." Raven grinned.

"We got more surprises." Marcie giggled. "Can we tell her now, Mommy? Please, I want to tell her."

"Not yet."

"Tell me what?"

"We've got a surprise for you." Mallory stood up. "Take my hand and close your eyes, Aunt Raven."

"Why?"

"So we can give you your surprise. Take my hands and close your eyes."

Amanda shrugged. "Better listen to them. They've worked hard to give you this surprise."

"OK, Mallory. This surprise better be good."

"Oh, it is." Marcie breathed. "Take my hand, too. Take my hand, too. I want to help."

She took each of the girl's hands. They led her out to her kitchen but kept walking. Then she heard the kitchen door open and felt a warm breeze on her face. The girls led her out on her deck.

"Don't open your eyes yet, Aunt Raven. When I count to three then you can open your eyes. OK?" Mallory instructed her as she let go of her hand.

Marcie kept hold and started giggling.

"OK."

"One." Both girls said at the same time. "Two. Three."

"Surprise!" A choir of voices shouted out.

She opened her eyes.

A huge cake set in the middle of the picnic table.

Hunter was there, and so were Gracie and Amanda's husband, Todd. Lydia was there as well. Raven felt a tug of guilt. All the people she'd been avoiding since she came back from New York. Apologies needed to be made. Later. "Oh, my goodness. This is great but it's not my birthday. What's this all about?"

Marcie giggled. "We know that. It's an I-love-you party."

"I've never heard of such a party."

Marcie tugged on Raven's hand so she bent down. Marcie wrapped her arms around her neck. "We love you, Auntie Raven. So much. And we're so happy you moved here."

Tears dripped down her cheeks as she lifted her niece up and held on tight. "I'm glad too. Marcie."

"Can we have cake now?" Marcie asked.

The adults laughed.

"I think that is a great idea." Raven looked at the others. "We want cake. We want cake."

The kids began chanting with her. "Cake. Cake."

Lydia picked up the cake knife and began slicing. "I made the cake. It's a black walnut cake with cream cheese icing. It is one of my specialties. Maybe I will bake it for the bakery."

"What bakery?" Amanda asked.

"Lydia and I are going to open a bakery." Raven answered. She looked at Lydia. "I'm sorry I didn't get back to you. I haven't felt well the last few days."

"Not a problem." Lydia gave her a sweet smile.

Her sister looked at her. "But you can't cook or bake."

Raven took a bite of the cake. Moist. Nutty.

Delicious. "But Lydia sure can."

Amanda took a big bite. "Oh, yes she can. I predict success if this is a sample of what you'll be selling."

"She's agreed to teach me how to bake—maybe even how to cook, too."

"Good luck with that." Todd said. "I've had your cooking."

More laughter.

When everyone was busy eating and talking, Raven slipped back into her kitchen for a moment alone to catch her breath. *Thank you, Father. I forgot for a while that I'm not alone in that barn anymore. You are with me always and there are people who love me. Who want to help me.*

The door opened behind her. Gracie rolled in. "A little overwhelming, huh?"

"Just a little but what a wonderful surprise."

"Are you OK? It seems you've been missing in action and everyone's been worried about you."

"Trust me, no one's been more worried than me. But I'm better now. Thanks to you."

"To me? What did I do?"

"I've been in the middle of a meltdown the past few days. But just a little bit ago, I remembered what you said about studying the Bible. When I picked it up, all those index cards you gave me fell out, so I started reading the verses. They were exactly what I needed."

Gracie smiled. "God is so amazing."

"Yes, He is."

"Care to share what was going on?"

"I'll tell you all about it at our session next week. I promise."

"OK. Then let's get back out there before everyone ends up in the kitchen. I'm sure everyone wants to talk with the guest of honor to make sure you're OK."

And she was OK. Now. Thanks to God. She may have more bad moments but now she knew Who to turn to.

They walked out. Her gaze met Hunter's. There was a question in his eyes. She hadn't talked to him or seen him since she came back from the book tour. She smiled at him and he smiled back but the smile didn't seem to reach his eyes.

Mallory set a box on the table. "We made up a box of your favorite things. Mommy says you can open it later. By yourself."

Marcie tugged on Raven's shirt. "I put my picture in it."

"And you certainly are one of my favorite things. Thank you very much, Mallory and Marcie, for this big surprise. I love my party."

Both girls beamed back at her.

Todd stood up. "And now it's time to go, girls. Dad's got to work in the morning while you get to play all day."

"Oh, Daddy. Not yet." Marcie whined.

"Yes, yet." Amanda stood up. "Daddy's your boss so move it, girls." She hugged Raven. "Are you sure you're OK?"

"Let's just say I'm much better now. Thanks to you. You have no idea how much I needed this."

"I'm glad you had fun. You deserve it." One more hug and Amanda and her family left.

"Time for me to go, too," Gracie said.

"Me, too. I will see you later, partner." Lydia walked off the deck.

"Hunter, if you take the wheelchair off the deck for me, I can get myself down." Gracie smiled at him.

"Oh, I can do better than that." He picked up the chair and Gracie together. He managed to get both of them off the deck in one piece. "I'll be back in a minute, Raven. Just seeing this beautiful lady to her car."

"Wow. I'm impressed." Gracie said with a laugh.

Raven was clearing off the deck when Hunter came back. He had a serious expression on his face.

"Thanks for coming, Hunter."

"I wasn't going to come."

She sat down and stared at him. "Why did you, then?"

"I decided I owed it to you to talk to you. Because that's what friends do. They talk to each other. They share their lives with each other. Do you agree with that?"

She looked down at the table, not wanting to meet his gaze. She had a feeling they were talking about more than his coming to the party. "Of course I agree, but sometimes it's not that simple."

He sat down opposite of her. "I want you to understand this is my fault, not yours."

She didn't like the direction this conversation was taking.

"I told you I wanted to be friends. And really I thought that was what I wanted. But the truth is I wanted more than that. I can see you're not ready for that. It's not your fault. You're still in the healing phase."

"But...I don't understand. Have I done something to upset you? I know we haven't talked in a few days, but I haven't talked to anyone. It wasn't just you."

"I know. Amanda was worried about you. That's why she put this little party together. She was hoping it would help."

"And it did. I do feel better and I'm so glad you came." She had the feeling they were breaking up. But how could that be when they weren't even a couple? "I know I've—"

"I need to feel that my friends—any of my friends—trust me. That they don't hide things from me."

Her stomach twisted. What did he think she was hiding from him? "And you don't think I trust you?"

He met her gaze. "I don't."

She wanted to look away, but she didn't because she didn't want him to go away. Hunter was important to her. "I do trust you, Hunter. And yes, I might not have shared everything with you, but it's not because I don't trust you. I do. Really."

"If you say so." He nodded and stood.

She put her hand over his. "Don't go. Not yet. I...I've always been a bit secretive. Even my ex-boss Marnie complained about it. It's something I need to change. And I'm working on it. Don't give up on me, Hunter."

He nodded. "I need to go."

"Does that mean you don't want to be my trainer any longer?"

30

Raven locked the door after Hunter left. She wasn't sure what to make of their conversation. It was obvious he wasn't happy with her. Had she lost her friend?

If she wanted a relationship with him—a real relationship—she owed it to him to be open and honest. She'd not outright lied, but she had omitted some personal things. Like her memories and her book. She sighed. Why did life have to be so complicated and confusing?

The favorites box Marcie and Mallory had given her sat on her kitchen table. She might as well take a look at what the girls put in it. She opened the flaps.

A picture of Marcie. A picture of Mallory. Then a picture of the whole family. She'd buy some frames so she could display them. A good reminder that she wasn't alone. That she had people who loved her.

A candy bar. Amanda knew her well. The peanut butter and chocolate concoction had always been a favorite. She pulled out a few more snacks, and then looked in the box.

Her heart raced as she picked up the last thing in the box.

The world turned wavy.

"It's been a while, Suzie Q. But don't worry I haven't forgotten you. I'll be coming for you. Soon. Just like the first time."

Then she was in her car. Driving. She stared at the text message on her phone.

MEET ME AT WV WELCOME CENTER. RIGHT NOW. IF YOU WANT MY STORY. IT HAS TO BE NOW OR NOT AT ALL. TRUST ME. YOU WANT THIS STORY.

Her fingers tapped on the steering wheel as she decided what to do. She rolled her eyes and sighed. A reporter didn't always get to decide when a story came up.

OK. 10 MINUTES.

Then she was standing by her car at the welcome center.

Another car pulled in beside her. She couldn't see the driver. A hoodie hid the face. A moment later the person leaned over and opened the passenger side of their car. "Raven?"

"That's me."

"Get in."

She shuddered. It's just the dark. She'd done scarier things in search of a story. She opened the door and sat down. The driver leaned toward her and lifted his hand. A needle. He had a needle. And…her mind went blank.

Just her imagination. Not real. Not real. She wasn't in a car. She was in her house. Alone. Not alone—God was with her. She wasn't with the monster, but she could hear his voice calling her Suzie Q. Her heart thumped. Another panic attack. Not real. She curled up into a ball.

She was back in the barn. As she clutched the silly little chocolate pastry the memories flooded back. Him taunting her. "If I say your name is Suzie Q then it is."

And no matter what memory, she saw the face of Charles Whitman. "It's not him. That's my mind playing tricks. It can't be him." Raven spoke it out loud.

The monster said, "It's been fun, Suzie Q."

She broke down sobbing and shaking as she remembered the horrible things the monster had done and said. Over and over, he'd told her how stupid she was. How worthless.

Another memory surfaced.

"Why are you here?"

"Because I'm a self-centered, celebrity-seeking narcissist."

"Much better, Suzie Q."

She glared. "Not my name."

Cattle prod.

"Your name is whatever I say it is, Suzie Q."

Cattle prod.

"Who am I?"

"A monster."

Cattle prod.

"I'm a patriot. I love America and you're a self-centered, celebrity-seeking reporter trying to ruin my country with your lies. Now who am I?"

"A patriot who loves America."

"Much better. Who are you?"

"A self-centered, celebrity-seeking reporter."

"I'm glad we understand each other."

Cattle prod. And again and again.

It wasn't one memory. They'd gone through the routine many times. But one thing remained constant. She was a bad reporter who told lies and he was a patriot. Almost as if he was trying to convince himself.

Why was he fixated on her as a reporter? How did he even know she was a reporter? These were all questions that needed answered, but not tonight.

The world straightened, and Raven opened her eyes. She was totally exhausted but she couldn't sleep in her house alone. Shaken, by the nightmare, Raven grabbed her keys.

Amanda wouldn't mind if she showed up at her house. In fact she'd probably be thrilled.

Raven walked outside.

Lydia was sitting on her own porch in a rocking chair. "Are you going somewhere, Raven?"

"I was, ah…going to Amanda's but, Lydia, would you mind if I sleep on your couch tonight?"

"Is everything all right?"

"Sometimes I get afraid of the dark. Of the night. This is one of those times. I was going to drive to Amanda's, but—"

"No need to drive there. Of course. Of course. Come on over. I would love to have a guest."

31

Bacon. And sausage. And biscuits. The aroma woke Raven up. She couldn't believe she'd actually slept through the night with no nightmares. It was almost as if now that her conscious mind had remembered the details of her kidnapping, it could no longer haunt her dreams.

She looked around the room. It was old-fashioned and so cute. She was covered with a gorgeous looking quilt. Had Lydia made it? She looked closer at the stitching. How could anyone do that by hand without a machine?

Amazing—not just the quilt but her.

She felt...she searched for a word...free. That's how she felt. Free—no longer trapped in that barn with the monster. She wouldn't let him steal her future the way he'd stolen those months from her. Raven walked into the kitchen. "Lydia, what are you doing?"

"I'm chust making us some breakfast."

"You didn't need to do that. I shouldn't have barged in last night."

"It was not barging, my friend. You needed a place to stay, and I was more than happy to provide it." She smiled at Raven. "I must say you look much better. Your business is your business. I'm chust glad I could help. And if you ever need to stay here again to feel safe, there is a key hidden in the flower box on the porch. Chust get the key and come in. Anytime."

"You are too kind to me, Lydia."

"Nonsense. We are partners, yes?"

"Yes."

They made plans to move forward with the bakery while they ate. Raven called and got an appointment for them to see the building in a few hours.

After the two ate a hearty breakfast—very hearty—Raven walked back to her house. She picked up the crumpled chocolate pastry, waiting for the now familiar anxiety to begin. It didn't. Instead she felt angry. How could someone have treated another human being the way she'd been treated? And he might be hurting someone else right now. She couldn't let that happen anymore. But how would she stop him when she couldn't even remember his face? It wasn't like her to get in a car with a stranger. She'd chosen to get in the car.

It was her own fault she'd been kidnapped.

Her heart thumped. Your peace, God. I need your peace. She took deep breaths. The world didn't turn wavy. Thank you.

There was only one reason she'd get in a car at night with a stranger. For a story. And he'd been fixated on the fact that she was a reporter. He'd told her she was trying to ruin the country with her lies while he was the good patriot. He'd known she was a reporter. And apparently, she'd written something he didn't like—probably a bit of an understatement considering he'd kidnapped her and tried to kill her.

"But you didn't kill me. Monster." She thought of the green glowing stick in her nightmare. "And I'm the one coming for you."

She picked up her phone. She scrolled through the names and hit one.

"Howdy, Raven. What's up?"

"Hi, Marnie. I was just thinking about you, so I decided to call. How are you?"

"I'm good. How about you?"

"It depends on what day you ask me that question. But I'm good today. I was wondering. I know we talked about this before and you said that I told you I might have a big story right before I disappeared."

"That's right."

"I don't suppose you remember what the story was about. Or who?"

"I don't remember because you didn't tell me. You like your secrets way too much, Raven. Even for a reporter."

Secrets. She thought of the books hidden in her bedroom. The fact that she hadn't told anyone that she was remembering things, except for Gracie. But even Gracie didn't know the extent of her memories. "I guess that's very true. I'm starting to think that's not the best way to be. Did you ever happen to come across my laptop at work?"

"No. Why all these questions?"

She started to say it wasn't important. Another secret? "I…uh…I'm not sure but I'm beginning to wonder if my kidnapping was as random as I thought."

"You think it could have something to do with your work?"

"I'm not sure, but it could be a possibility. What do you think?"

"Anything's possible, I suppose. But I don't think

so."

"Why not?"

"I don't know. I mean you just finished up with that series about the primaries. It's not like you wrote anything bad about the candidates. As far as I knew, you weren't really working on anything else that might make someone that mad."

"So you don't think it's probable."

"Probably not."

It was good to hear that Marnie thought it was random. Which was better? Random, or her as the target? Raven decided the idea that she was the target was definitely more terrifying.

Time to go look at a bakery.

~*~

"It's perfect, yes?" Lydia asked with a huge smile on her face. "We can turn this into a bakery without much problem at all."

"I agree but—"

"Then I will let the owner know we would like to rent it. He said we would have to pay for our own renovations but that in return he would give us a few free months with no rent."

"That's nice of him. Lydia, I love this idea but it's moving a little too fast for me."

"I see. So you don't want to open the bakery."

"I do want to, but I don't know anything about fixing this place up or anything like that."

"Not a problem. I know people who can help with that. We Amish are very handy people, yes?"

"That's the thing, Lydia. You'll be baking. You

know people to fix it up. Why do you need me?"

"Because you are my partner."

"But what am I supposed to do?"

"Be my partner."

32

Raven sat outside on her deck staring at her laptop. What was she was working on at the time of her disappearance? It wasn't just the memories from her disappearance that were messed up. She couldn't seem to remember the articles she'd written about the upcoming election either. The monster may have been triggered by any of her stories. She'd certainly upset a few people with past columns.

But she couldn't focus on every story she'd ever written so first she'd try to figure out what she was working on at the time. It might not have anything to do with her disappearance. But then again, it might. And unfortunately, she didn't have that laptop any longer to look anything up. Did the monster have it? Probably.

She was almost sure it had been in the car the night she disappeared. Had he destroyed it? If he still had it, could she access it remotely? Did she even have her computer set up for remote access? It was a long shot but she'd never know if she didn't try. She wasn't a hacker. But she needed the user name and password to access the computer. Going to the settings on this computer, she tried to remember what they were. Frustrated, she stared for a while. And then it came to her.

The cloud.

She didn't need access to her old computer to get to her files. It was all backed up on the cloud. Why hadn't she remembered that before?

Ten minutes later she was staring at the files from her old computer.

And she was still frustrated. Not one of the files seemed to be about some big story that she was pursuing at the time. She clicked her fingers on her keyboard, still staring at the files. Now what? She'd been positive that finding out the big story would lead her to the monster.

Back to the beginning. She scrolled through each file. Her cursor moved from the As to the Bs to the Cs. And then she stopped at the Es. Her email files.

Who knew? Maybe she'd find something in one of them that might hold a clue as to what she was working on. From the beginning of the year forward, she meticulously opened every file and read the contents. As she scrolled through, her pulse began to race.

And then she found it. She went back to the beginning and read it again.

Ms. Marks,

I have a secret that I've never shared with anyone else. Like many secrets it could destroy lives. Not just mine but the life of someone very important. I don't know if you're the right person to tell but I think you might be.

I read your story about that coach who was seducing his players and embezzling money from the team. You seemed to really care about the people that coach hurt. And you helped those people to get justice.

That's what I care about now.

Justice.

If the secret comes out my life may be destroyed but if it stays a secret even more lives could be destroyed. If you're interested in writing a story about my secret, contact me.

Sydney Bartrum

After rereading it several times, she looked for more emails from Sydney. None. So then she searched for emails she'd sent to Sydney. And she found her reply.

Sydney,

Of course, I'm interested in your story, but I need more information before I decide if it's a real story. I'm sending you my phone number so we talk and set up a time to meet. I'll be glad to come to you—where ever you are.

Raven L. Marks

That was it. No more emails to or from Sydney. Had he changed his mind and decided it wasn't worth it to ruin his life to expose this supposed terrible secret where she'd agreed to meet with someone at the West Virginia Welcome Center? It must have been Sydney. Was Sydney her kidnapper? Or was it the person Sydney wanted to expose? She copied Sydney's email address and then went to her present email program and pasted into an email.

Sydney,

I know it's been a long time since we were in contact with each other. For my part, I had to take some time off work due to a medical condition. But I'm ready to get to work on your story again. I would love to hear what you

wanted to tell me.
   Please contact me as soon as you get this.
   Thank you,
   Raven L. Marks

She hit send and then sat staring at the screen, praying for a quick response. After five minutes, she realized she was being ridiculous. A look at her watch told her it was time for her self-defense class.

33

As she walked toward the building, Raven thought of the conversation with Hunter. At the beginning, it sounded as if he was breaking up with her which was ridiculous since they weren't actually dating. By the end it sounded as if he'd changed his mind—sort of.

She still had a chance to show him how much he meant to her.

But he was right. One couldn't really have a relationship with someone—whether as friends or something more— if one kept secrets. And right now she seemed to have a lot of them.

But that would stop—soon.

Hunter was talking to the receptionist. He made his way toward Raven with a smile. "How are you today? Did you sleep well?"

Just seeing that smile made her happy. He was friendly and just making small talk. How was she supposed to tell him about the flood of memories she'd had after he left last night? More secrets. "How about you?"

"Like a baby." He didn't seem to notice that she hadn't answered his question. "You ready? Great. We'll do some warm-ups and then running. I know how much you love the running." He held the door open to the gym.

She walked through.

Forty-five minutes later Hunter handed her a bottle of water. "Great work out. I can't believe how much you've improved in such a short time."

"It doesn't seem that short to me, but thanks." She took a long drink of water.

"See you next week."

She took a deep breath. She promised herself she'd tell him all about her memories then. And maybe even the book. "Actually, I was hoping I could cook dinner for you. For us. Not pizza but real food. I'm pretty rusty at the cooking thing but if you're willing to take a chance."

His smile faded.

Not good.

She rushed on. "I...I ...I want to talk to you. I need to tell you some things. About what's been going on with me. Unless you don't want to know."

"I'm not trying to pressure you into anything. After last night I thought we'd just stick to training sessions for the time being."

"It's important, Hunter. I have things I need to tell you."

He looked at her for a moment then nodded. "Sure, let's do it."

"Do you like Italian?"

"Who doesn't?"

"Perfect."

When she got back to her house, she checked her email. Sydney Bartrum had responded.

I'm sorry to inform you that Sydney passed away last

year. I'm her sister, so I'm still handling email for her though I will be closing down the account soon.

Your email was a bit of a shock and I really have no idea what she might have wanted to tell you so I'm afraid I can't really be of help to you. But thank you for following up with her.

Fran Baker

Her? Sydney was a woman. And she was dead.
Raven's fingers clicked on the keyboard.

Dear Fran,

I'm so sorry about the loss of your sister but I really do have more questions for you. She wanted me to tell a story— her story. She seemed to think it was an important one that needed told.

I understand that you don't know what it was either but I would still love to meet with you so we could talk and I could get to know a little about Sydney through you. Together we might be able to figure out her story and share it the way she wanted.

I will be more than happy to come to where you live. Please let me know as soon as possible so I can make arrangements.

Raven L. Marks.

She sent the message and immediately began a search for Sydney Bartrum on the Internet. It was a little difficult since she still didn't know where Sydney was from. But she typed in the name and waited to see what would come up.

She scrolled through the choices until one caught her eye. An obituary. She opened it. No real details other than the date and place. Both made her a bit more attentive.

The funeral was held in Marietta but said she'd lived in Columbus. She must have been from the Marietta area which would explain why she'd contacted Raven in the first place.

But even more interesting was the date of her death.

May fourth of the previous year.

The day before Raven disappeared.

34

Raven was a bit jittery about the whole investigative reporting thing, but something inside kept telling her to learn more about Sydney Bartrum and her secret. It couldn't be a coincidence that the woman had died the day before Raven's disappearance. So Raven decided to take a trip to Marietta.

Unfortunately, she'd had to cancel another session with Gracie yet again. She'd called to let Gracie know with a promise to make it up to her. In an effort to be more open and less secretive, she'd told her that she was working on a story that couldn't wait. Gracie had been shocked but understanding. Raven admitted she'd thought she'd never work as a reporter again and promised to give Gracie more details later.

Raven was early. She pulled into the same restaurant parking lot she was supposed to meet Marnie at the night she'd disappeared. She willed herself back to that night. Had she got here? Or had she driven to the West Virginia Welcome Center where her car had been found? She remembered getting into a car with a stranger but not the location. Maybe she'd go over to the Welcome Center before she left the area.

She should have come last night. The dark might

have triggered a memory. Details. That's what she needed. More details. Up to this point all she could remember was getting into a car. The man wore a hoodie that hid his face.

Sydney was a woman, so Raven hadn't got into her car. Besides Sydney was already dead when Raven met the person. Sighing, she stepped out of her car—the same car she'd been in that night. She stood outside the door, waiting to see if being here brought on any new memories.

"Excuse me."

Panicked, Raven swirled around ready to fight. Nobody would hurt her again. She leaned against the car and readied to kick him.

The man stepped back, clearly surprised at her reaction. He held his hands up as if to surrender. "Sorry, I didn't mean to scare you."

She took a deep breath. "What do you want?"

"Just a few dollars, so I can get something to eat."

She dug in her purse and pulled out a five.

"Thanks so much." He headed to the fast food place across the street and went in.

She still stood grounded, pleased that her first reaction had been to defend herself. Of course, Hunter was always telling her the best response was to leave the situation. Even though she agreed, it was good to know she'd defend herself if necessary. But Hunter was right—it was better that it hadn't been necessary.

She walked into the restaurant.

The hostess was at a little podium.

"I'm supposed to meet someone. Fran Baker."

"She's already here. Follow me."

After they introduced themselves and food was ordered, Raven smiled. "I really appreciate you meeting me."

"Oh, you're very welcome. I needed to come here anyway and check on Sydney's...burial site."

"So you don't live here?"

"No. I live in West Virginia. Charleston. But Sydney and I were born here. Our dad got a job in Charleston when we were young so that's where we grew up. But my parents were buried here and so when Sydney died, I had her buried beside them."

"I see. So the obituary said she lived in Columbus."

"True. About six months before she died, she abruptly quit her job in Charleston and moved to Columbus. She was working part time and going to school at Ohio State. She was going to be a teacher." Fran's eyes filled with tears. "She would have been a good teacher."

"I'm sure she would have been. So what did she do before she moved there? What did she do in Charleston?"

"Oh, she worked at a restaurant. A fancy restaurant where she made great tips. I thought she really liked it there. And she had a boyfriend and everything. And suddenly one day she up and quits and moves to Ohio. It was surprising but she seemed really happy every time I talked to her."

"That's nice. Did she quit because she broke up with the boyfriend?"

"No, they were still dating even though it was long distance. According to Syd he was actually planning on moving to Columbus to be with her before she died."

She nodded. "So how did she die?"

Fran bit down on her lip. "It was a stupid accident.

Really stupid."

"A car accident?"

She shook her head. "No. She was doing her laundry. Apparently some of the tenants in the apartment building liked to hang their laundry on the roof. That's what she was up there doing and somehow she fell."

"Oh, how awful."

"A tragic accident. She must have tripped or something and then lost her balance. She always was clumsy."

But was it an accident? How could the woman who wanted to tell her a secret just happen to die on the day before Raven disappeared? And in such a bizarre way? "And you don't have any idea what she might have wanted to tell me?"

"I can't come up with anything."

"Do you think she might have told her boyfriend?"

"I was wondering the same thing, so I called him. He did say that he felt as if something was bothering her, but he had no idea what. Every time he tried to talk to her about it, she'd just say it was in the past and she didn't want to talk about it."

But she'd wanted to tell Raven.

Their lunch came and the conversation turned to more pleasant things. They walked out of the restaurant together. As they said their good-byes, Raven asked, "What was the name of the restaurant where Sydney worked in Charleston?"

"It's called The Capital Dining Room. Because it's near the state capital building. Why?"

"Oh, no reason, just curious."

35

Raven got on the highway but instead of heading north, she drove south toward Charleston. She couldn't quite explain why she was going, only that it felt like the right thing.

She'd spend the night there, find out what she could. Then she'd drive back early to have the day to prepare for the dinner with Hunter. Her plan was to come clean—to tell him about her recovered memories and the book. She wanted him to know he was special and that she did trust him. She thought maybe spaghetti or baked ziti rather than the lasagna she'd considered. It would take less time.

Why was she even heading to Charleston? As an investigative reporter, one had to let the leads take one to the story she reasoned. Sydney's boyfriend felt she was hiding something but wasn't sure what it could be. Maybe one of her coworkers knew.

Raven knew from her own experience she often shared bits and pieces of her life with the people she worked with. She was hoping Sydney did the same.

She found the Capitol Dining Room without a problem. And just as Fran had said, the golden dome of West Virginia's capitol building was in view as she walked into the restaurant.

She'd barely made it through the door when the hostess was there with a smile. "Good afternoon. How many?"

"Actually, I'm not here to eat."

"Oh." The smile faltered. "Then how can I help you?"

"I...uh...I'm a reporter from Ohio, and I'm looking into a story that involves Sydney Bartrum. I know she used to work here, and I wanted to talk to some of her coworkers."

"Of course, we know... knew Sydney. We loved Sydney. We were all so sad when...well you know what happened."

"Were you close to her?"

"Not really."

Of course not. It couldn't be that easy.

"She worked the afternoon shift and I work the day shift. So we'd see each other but..." She shrugged. "You know what? It's almost time for shift change so her crew's back in the employee lounge if you want to talk to them."

"That would be great."

Her smile was back. "Follow me."

They walked through the nearly empty restaurant except for a few customers sitting by the windows. The hostess opened the door marked employees only. "Hey, y'all. This woman is doing a story on Sydney and would like to talk to you." Without waiting for a response, she turned and left.

"What kind of story?" A woman with short brown hair asked.

"I'm not sure yet." Might as well be truthful.

The woman nodded. "Well, Sydney was a nice person. So sweet. Always willing to help out when you'd get swamped in your own section. You could count on her if you needed to switch a shift for some reason."

A young man nodded. "That's so true. And she was a great server. She could carry six glasses of water at a time without a tray."

The woman laughed. "Except that time when a customer stood up just as she was passing."

The three at the table started laughing. "True. But she got a huge tip out of it anyway."

"Yes, she did."

"She sounds like a gem." Raven said and meant it. "Were you surprised when she quit so suddenly?"

"I certainly was." The young man responded. "One day she's talking about moving in with her boyfriend, and the next day she tells me it's her last shift. I was dumbfounded."

"Yeah, me too." The brown-haired woman agreed.

Raven noticed the third person at the table wasn't saying much so she looked directly at her. "Did you know Sydney?"

The door opened before she could answer. The hostess yelled in. "Two minutes until shift change, people."

The young man smiled. "Sorry, we gotta go."

"No problem."

The two of them walked out. The third woman at the table didn't move. Instead, she motioned for Raven to sit. "Sydney was my best friend. Not just work friends but real-life friends. She helped me get my job here."

"So what do you know about her deciding to quit?"

"A lot. But I can't talk now."

"It's important."

"I know it is. Can you wait until I go on break?"

"Absolutely."

The young woman obviously knew something. But if Raven left now, she could get home tonight.

An hour later the woman walked back in the lounge. "You're still here?"

"I am."

"Sorry, I had to get my shift started but I have a few minutes now."

"I understand. I'm Raven Marks."

"Jenet. Sydney really was my best friend."

"So what do you know that I need to know?"

She looked at Raven. "Something happened. I'm not sure I should tell you. Why are you asking these questions so long after she died?"

"Fair question. I only recently became aware of Sydney. She emailed me about a secret she thought other people needed to know. When I tried to follow through with it, I found out she'd passed away."

"Yeah, I always found that whole thing suspicious."

"Why?"

She looked flustered. "People don't usually fall off a flat roof by accident. It just seemed odd to me."

"Do you think maybe she jumped off the roof rather than fell?"

"No. Absolutely not. She wouldn't do that. Ever."

"So you think someone might have pushed her?"

Jenet met her gaze. "I only know Sydney wouldn't have jumped on her own. And that she wasn't clumsy enough to fall off a roof without some help."

"OK. What do you know about why she quit?"

"She served at a catered event one evening. A few

days before Halloween. The next day she told me something. And a week later, she quit."

"What did she tell you?"

"That one of the bigwigs started coming on to her. She flirted back of course. That's how we get the big tips. Anyway, when she left, he apparently followed her." She stopped.

"And…"

Jenet met her gaze. "And he tried to put the moves on her. When she resisted, he raped her."

Raven wished she'd been more surprised. Things like this happened way too often. "Why didn't she report it to the police?"

"I tried to get her to do that, but she was too afraid. He's an important person."

"Who was it?"

Jenet shook her head. "She wouldn't tell me. All I know was that he was at that catered event at the Capital Building the week of Halloween. He apparently contacted her and apologized to her afterward."

"How nice of him."

"Yeah, that's what I thought. Along with the apology came some big money, according to Syd."

"Enough money for her to quit and go to school."

"Exactly."

"Are you sure you don't have any idea who it was?"

"No. I don't even know who attended."

"Do you remember the date of the event?"

She thought back. "I think it was the Tuesday before Halloween, but I'm not sure. I bowl on Tuesdays which is why I didn't help cater it."

"I will be looking into this. Thanks so much for

telling me."

She stood up. "I need to go, but I hope you can get some justice for Sydney."

"I'll try."

"Be careful." Jenet warned her. "I think this man could be very dangerous."

Raven walked out to her car with Jenet's warning echoing. If the man who raped Sydney was the same man who'd kidnapped her, Jenet was right.

He was a very dangerous man.

36

Charles Whitman stared at the computer monitor. He'd paid a lot of money to have access to certain tracking programs that revealed more information about people than they'd be comfortable sharing. Being a presidential candidate had its perks.

Raven Marks was still alive and well. And apparently not minding her own business. He'd started monitoring her credit cards and debit card transactions as soon as Robert had located her. As long as she stayed in some little town called Charm, he wasn't worried. But today, she'd left her little hideaway and gone to Marietta. And even more interesting, a search of her emails revealed she'd reached out to Sydney. Sydney's sister had emailed Suzie Q back and the two met in Marietta. After that she got gas in Charleston. He had to assume that she was talking to the people who knew Sydney before she'd moved to Columbus. But Sydney had assured him that she'd told no one about him.

Did he believe her?

She'd been begging for her life at the time so she might not have been completely truthful. Sydney admitted to contacting a reporter, but she'd promised that she hadn't given any details and that she would never contact anyone again. Charles was pretty sure that was the truth, but that didn't mean Raven Marks couldn't find out more. She was too good of a reporter.

And that made her dangerous. It was obvious that she was on his trail. That made Raven a problem he couldn't afford. Any scandals at this point in the race could be devastating. A few more months and he could—no would—be the next President. But he would need to take care of the Raven problem. He couldn't trust anyone else to do it.

Where would she land for the night? Having his own private plane gave him the luxury of coming and going without the relentless press being able to follow his every move. There were plenty of small, private airfields across the country where you didn't have to file a flight plan. His plane was big enough to carry a small motorcycle so he could slip in and out of places without anyone ever knowing he'd been there.

Tonight he'd take care of the Raven problem permanently.

37

Raven's mind raced as she made her way back toward Ohio. Could the man who raped Sydney be the same man who'd kidnapped her? It seemed odd but the timing tied everything together. Somehow he must have found out that Sydney contacted her. He could have pushed her off that roof, and then kidnapped Raven in Marietta. Whoever the monster was, he was dangerous—very dangerous.

It was such a farfetched idea that even she had a hard time believing. And there was absolutely no proof. The rational thing would be to forget about all of it. Go on with her life. Open the bakery with Lydia. Hopefully, start a relationship with Hunter and then live happily ever after.

Sydney was dead so Raven couldn't help her by pursuing the story.

There was just one problem. A big problem. If she chose to leave it alone, then the monster was free to hurt more women. Monsters who weren't caught did terrible things as long as they could get away with it.

Raven didn't think she could live with that knowledge.

He might even have another victim right that moment.

Her eyes drooped and she swerved. Time to find a room. At least she'd made it to Ohio. She pulled off the first exit and found a hotel.

The clerk asked a few questions and then entered information into the computer.

At his prompting, Raven handed over her credit card.

38

Raven fell asleep almost as soon as her head hit the pillow. Her dreams were formless, dark, scary...

She sat up in bed, her senses on high alert.

A smoke alarm blared. Fire? In the motel? She turned on the light, jumped out of bed and stood in the middle of the room. She took a deep breath but didn't smell any smoke.

Maybe it was a false alarm.

The clock read 4: 45. Even if there wasn't a fire she probably couldn't get back to sleep. She put on clothes and grabbed her purse and keys. Might as well drive home. She could take a nap later while the lasagna was baking. She opened the door and walked outside. Sleepy, half-dressed people milled around. She walked up to the closest person. "What's going on?"

"I'm not—"

The clerk came out of the lobby. "Everything's fine. It was a false alarm. Someone pulled the fire alarm. You can all go back to bed. I am so sorry about this."

"It's not your fault." Raven assured him. "But I'm heading out. I left the key card in my room. Do I need to do anything else?"

"Don't worry about a thing, I'll take care of it."

The others started going back in their rooms.

Raven walked to her car and hit the unlock button on her remote.

"Oh, miss." The clerk called.

She looked back at him.

"The manager said I was to refund anyone who left."

"You don't have to do that."

"It's already been approved. I just need your signature on the receipt."

"That's so nice."

While Raven was in the lobby, she got a large cup of coffee. Between the coffee and loud music, she shouldn't have a problem staying awake. The music blared as she started her car.

She took a sip of coffee before putting the car in gear. Too hot. She quickly set it back to cool off then took the lid off. That would make it cool quicker. The highway was mostly empty as she drove along. Everyone else was at home safe and sound, sleeping.

Which is what she should be doing. Instead she'd spent the day rushing from place to place. And yes, she had some answers but not the big answer.

Who was the monster?

The truth was even if she discovered his identity, she probably couldn't do anything about it since she had no proof. And it wasn't like anyone would believe her faulty memory. She knew she wouldn't. But at least she had a better understanding of what had happened to her and why. Just not the who. And that would have to be enough for now.

Just like the Bible said, there was a time for everything under the sun. A time to grieve and a time to dance. It was her time to dance.

Life was good. She had friends. A best-selling book. And Hunter. She didn't exactly have Hunter. She couldn't put a name to what they were. Yet. She smiled. But whatever it was, it made her happy, just the same.

Thump. Thump.

Was there something wrong with the car? She turned down the music so she could listen. More thumps and then she felt it. A flat tire. Great—just what she needed. There went her plans for a nap.

She pulled off the side of the road but didn't get out of the car. The whole thing was spooky. A flat tire in the middle of nowhere and still dark. Oh well, she couldn't just sit here.

She stepped out of the car and walked around. And there it was—the front passenger tire—flat as a pancake. And she hadn't even thought of renewing her auto club membership.

She'd just have to change it herself.

She took a deep breath. I can do this. I can. She pulled her key out of the ignition and then opened her trunk. She stared at the spare as she shook her head. First a fake fire alarm and then a flat tire. Could anything else happen between now and when she got home?

Her pulse sped up—and her breathing. Anxiety attack—the last thing she needed right now. She gripped the trunk lid. "God is with me. God gives me a sound mind, not fear."

And then she could almost hear Hunter telling her, "If a situation feels wrong, leave. Just leave."

Down the road, she saw a headlight—one headlight. And heard the motorcycle. And then she remembered—the monster used a motorcycle when he visited her.

Hunter's voice. "Just leave."

Without another thought, she ran off the highway and across the field. Trees were ahead of her. Putting all her energy, she sprinted toward the trees. She told herself she was being paranoid but so be it.

And then she was in the trees. She stayed hidden as she watched the motorcycle pull up behind her car. The man didn't hesitate. He walked quickly to her side of the car and opened it. Then he started looking around. For her? He was probably just a Good Samaritan wanting to help a stranded motorist.

He could probably change her tire for her. Maybe she should go back. If she did, she wouldn't lose all that much time.

He walked back to his motorcycle but didn't get on. She still had time to go back, let him help her. He stood by his motorcycle, looking around.

A chill went up her back.

Was he looking for her?

Then he started jogging across the field—toward her.

39

The moment Raven saw what he was doing, she turned and ran in the opposite direction, weaving through the trees. Thank you, Hunter for making her run and run and run some more. She'd hated it at the time but was glad she'd stuck to the regime. Thanks to all that training, she sprinted far ahead of the man. But he could still be back there. Somewhere.

Could he really be after her?

It seemed farfetched. He was probably just taking a bathroom break off the highway, but she wasn't going to wait around to see. She kept running. Finally houses came into view. As she ran out of the woods and into a housing community, she finally stopped and turned back. Breathing hard, she looked behind her.

No one. At least she couldn't see anyone. But that didn't mean he wasn't out there. Watching her. Waiting. She rolled her eyes, sure she'd overreacted to the situation.

Only one house had lights on at this crazy time of the morning. She jogged over to it. Please God, let them help me. She rang the buzzer. A moment later, a voice asked through a closed door. "Who is it?"

"I need help. Please. Please let me in."

The door opened. A woman stood there. "What's

wrong?"

"I had a flat tire. Out on the highway. I didn't know what to do. I ran through the woods and ended up here."

"Oh my goodness, that's awful." The woman opened the screen. "Come in. I have a phone you can use."

"I'm not from this area and I don't have auto club, so I didn't know who to call."

"Not a problem. Actually, I'm sure my husband can change the tire for you. Let me go wake him up."

"Don't do that. I can probably change it myself. I just got a little freaked out with it being dark and everything."

"I don't blame you for that. But no reason not to let my husband help."

"What's going on?" Her husband walked in the room.

"She has a flat tire. Over on the highway. "Can you help her?"

"Of course." He held up a finger. "Just give me a few minutes."

"Are you sure? I don't want to be a bother."

He smiled. "Not a problem. Just give me a few minutes."

After he left, the woman said, "My goodness. You must be exhausted after that hike. It's more than two miles through the woods to the highway. Would you like some breakfast?"

Raven smiled. The woman reminded her of Lydia, ready to help at a moment's notice. And always wanting to feed her. "That's not necessary. Thank you so much for letting me in. A lot of people wouldn't have done it."

"Well, I'm not a lot of people. Jesus said when we help those in need we're helping him. So that's the way I try to live. Breakfast?"

"I'm fine."

"I'm sure you are but it'll be ready in a few minutes."

40

Raven checked her makeup.

Dinner for Hunter would be ready soon. She planned to share everything with him, despite being so tired she could barely keep her eyes open. The doorbell buzzed just as she walked back in the living room. She peeked out the window. Hunter was right on time. She hurried over and opened the door. "You're quite the punctual one, aren't you?"

"Sorry, it's my military training."

"Nothing to be sorry about. I like it. Want some coffee?"

He held up a bottle of wine. "I brought this. It goes with Italian."

"Oh, that's sweet, but I need coffee. You're free to enjoy the wine with dinner."

"Nah, we can save it for another day."

That sounded like a promise to continue their friendship. Her heart lifted. She pointed at his other hand. He had a small brown bag. "What's that?"

"It's part of the conversation. Later."

"So you're not going to show me now?"

"Later." He followed her to the kitchen.

She smiled at him. "I didn't sleep much last night. I need the caffeine."

"Why not?"

"Like you said it's for the conversation. Later." She slipped a coffee pod in the machine and hit the large button. "It won't make a whole lot of sense because it's the end of the story not the beginning." She removed her cup. "Sure you don't want some coffee?"

"No thanks. I'll just have some pop if you have it."

"Check out the fridge. There's several choices." She took a sip of coffee.

"Something smells good."

"Lasagna." She walked to the refrigerator and pulled out a bowl. "And salad."

"Perfect."

"And the rest of Lydia's walnut cake."

"Maybe we should start with dessert."

"No way, not after I worked so hard on the lasagna. Want to eat outside?"

Once everything was outside and the food on their plates, thoughts raced around in Raven's mind. Hunter was so good, so honest, and so trusting. What would he think when she told him her secrets? And more importantly, how would he feel about her?

He took a bite of lasagna.

She wasn't really hungry but took a bite anyway. "I...think I made a mistake."

"Not at all. It tastes great."

She smiled. "Not about the lasagna, Hunter. Me. I've made some wrong choices in my life lately."

"So what if you made a mistake. It's not a big deal. Everyone does. So what did you do?" He laid down his fork. "You can tell me anything."

"You were right the other night. I have been keeping secrets. Not just from you, but from everybody. Even Amanda."

"So will you tell me these deep, dark secrets, now?"

"I'm just trying to figure out the best way to tell you." She nibbled on a bite of lettuce. "Everything."

He took hold of her hand. "It'll be fine, Raven. I can't imagine that you've done anything all that horrible that you should be this upset about it."

"I hope that you'll feel the same way in a little bit. I...I...this is so hard. I'm not even sure where to start but I want you to know I didn't tell you any of this before not because I didn't trust you. I do trust you...very much so. I think it's a habit I picked up as a reporter and it just sort of infiltrated my whole life."

"OK." He took a huge bite of the lasagna then gave her a thumbs up.

"I've been remembering things about my abduction—for a while. Actually as soon as I moved here, I started to remember bits and pieces Things that happened to me while...while I was kidnapped."

"That's what you wanted. Why would you hide it?"

Truth time. "I'm not completely sure. It just...the memories...made me feel dirty. Ashamed."

He set down his fork. "Whatever happened to you, Raven, it wasn't your fault. You have nothing to be ashamed of. If you don't want to share the details, you don't have to. That's certainly your right."

"The very first night here, I had this dream about being chained up in a barn. I wasn't sure if it was a dream or a memory. I decided it was a dream."

"And now?"

"And now, I'm sure it wasn't a dream. It was a memory. That's really why I went to West Virginia a few weeks ago. It wasn't just a road trip for fun. It was to see if I could remember more."

"And did you?"

"Not then, but yes, I've remembered more. Actually, a lot more."

"Do you remember who kidnapped you?"

"Sort of."

"That's great, Raven. We can find this monster and have him prosecuted for what he did to you."

She shook her head. "Probably not. I remember him but can't remember his face. Besides my memories are so jumbled and confusing they wouldn't hold up in court."

"That's too bad, but still I think you need to share what you do remember with the sheriff investigating the case. It could help. That's the thing about an investigation. It's impossible to know what tiny piece of the puzzle will complete the picture."

"That makes sense, but the problem is I don't trust my memories. Things still get all mixed up in my mind. Sometimes I'm not sure what's real and not real."

"What do you mean?"

"This is going to sound bizarre, but I was watching the presidential debates on TV, and I became convinced that one of the candidates was the man who abducted me. Suddenly the monster had a face—a famous face."

"That is strange."

"Then when I went down to West Virginia, I was with the sheriff, Matthew Borden. Then I became convinced he was the man. I could see him perfectly as the monster." She looked at him. "See what I mean about not being able to trust my memories."

"I could see how that could be a problem."

"One of the reasons I went to Berkeley Springs is that I found out that the presidential candidate I'd fixated on was actually from the area where I was found. I couldn't ignore that. I had to check it out. It makes no sense but still it haunted me."

"I can understand how that could be the case. Who's the man?"

"Charles Whitman, III."

His eyes widened. "Oh...you mean the next President of the United States. That Charles Whitman." He took another bite of the lasagna. "Do you really think he's the one who kidnapped you?"

"Not at all. I know how bizarre all this is. I only told you to demonstrate how I can't trust my memories. And why it's so confusing. Gracie and I talked about it. She explained how your mind can fill in unknown information with something that is known."

"One of the reasons why eyewitnesses to a crime are so unreliable."

His plate was empty. "Want some more lasagna?"

"Not after that giant piece, but I'll take some home if you don't mind. It's very good."

"Thank you, and you can take some home."

"And I would love a piece of Lydia's cake."

After she cut a piece of cake for each of them, she continued, "Anyway, something started bothering me a few days ago. One of the things I can remember is that the monster kept telling me my news stories were lies. And that I was a horrible person because I was reporting lies. He talked about how bad I was because I was a reporter."

"That's pretty specific, Raven."

"That's what I thought, too. That's when I began to

wonder if my kidnapping was connected to a story I was working on."

"Makes sense." He swallowed a bite of cake. "Lydia knows how to bake."

"Yes, she does. Anyway, I didn't have my old laptop, but I remembered I backed up all my stuff to the cloud. Even my emails."

"Did you find something?"

"That's why I went to Marietta yesterday, and then ended up in Charleston. I found an email from this woman named Sydney Bartrum who said she had an important story I needed to tell. When I tried to contact her, I found out she died." She paused. "The day before I was kidnapped."

"Wow. That can't be a coincidence." He took another big bite of the cake.

"That's what I thought. I ended up talking to her sister. I found out not long before she died, she quit her job out of the blue and moved to Columbus to go to school."

"How'd she die?"

"They ruled it as accidental. She fell from the roof of her apartment."

"You're kidding me." He set down his fork.

"I'm not. Also, the sister was shocked to discover the amount of money she had in her bank account. Almost one hundred thousand dollars. The sister had no idea how she could have that much money. She worked as a server before she quit to go to school."

"Someone paid her off?"

"That's what I was thinking so I drove to Charleston where she worked at The Capital Dining Room, a very fancy restaurant that caters to the political crowd. I talked to her best friend who told me that Sydney was raped but was afraid to come forward. Shortly after that she quit her job. Of course, Sydney refused to tell the name of her rapist."

"It's never that easy, but that's a lot of information. You must have been a very good reporter. So what will you do now?"

"What can I do? First of all, it's all hearsay and second of all, I don't even have a clue who the man is. And no actual proof."

"But do you believe it was the same man who abducted you?"

"Don't you?"

"I'd say there's a pretty strong reason to believe that." Hunter said as he took a sip of his soda.

"Yeah, me too."

"Do you have any ideas about figuring out who it is?"

"A few, but I'm not finished baring my soul yet."

"More secrets?"

"One is a secret, and one just happened. This morning. Which is why I'm exhausted. Which would you like to hear first?"

"I love secrets but first I sort of have a secret of my own." He handed her the package he'd carried in.

It was a shape that looked like it could be a book. She an inkling what might be in it. "I think I might be busted."

He shrugged. "Maybe. Go ahead and open it."

She did.

"*Unsinkable* by Jane Doe. It's about you, right?"

She nodded. "I'm Jane Doe. How did you know?"

"I saw one of the interviews, and the story was so similar to yours I bought a copy. The more I read the more convinced I was that it was you. Even though you did a great job disguising yourself during the interview."

"Why didn't you ask me?"

"Why didn't you tell me?"

"I have no idea. As I said, the more I remember the more shame I feel. I believe God wanted me to write the story to help other people, so I did. But the thought of sharing such personal things with people I know, it sort of freaked me out."

"There's no reason to feel that way at all. The book is wonderful."

"Thank you." Tears filled her eyes. "It made sense at the time. Now it just seems silly. Especially considering it's always been my dream to be a writer. And here I have a bestseller, and I'm keeping it a secret."

"A bestseller, huh? That's great."

"Are you mad at me?"

"For what?"

"For keeping it a secret. For not telling you."

"I admit that I wished you'd told me about it. But I'm sure you thought you were doing the right thing when you decided to keep it a secret." He tapped the name Jane Doe on the cover. "I guess the plan was for you to stay anonymous."

"When I first talked to my agent, I said it was because the story wasn't about me, but about God. And that's still true. But I've come to realize I'm still afraid. Not just afraid of the monster who kidnapped me, but afraid people will look at me differently if they know the truth of what happened to me."

"That's totally understandable, but I think you're wrong about that."

She shook her head. "I've been so afraid. All the

time. Every time I see a stranger, I think he could be the monster. If someone slows down as they walk past my house, I'm afraid. I have to force myself to leave the house. Then I'm afraid when I come back."

"You've been through a lot so it's totally understandable."

"No. It's not understandable. It goes against everything I say in the book. About trusting God. I felt like a fraud. But all that changed two nights ago. I had a breakthrough. With God. I'm trusting Him, now."

"I think you're one of the most courageous people I know — if not the most. Courage isn't about not being afraid. It's about acting in spite of the fear. And that's what I see you do every day. You fought your way back to walking. You're fighting your way back to recovery. You fight every day to rebuild your life into what you want it to be."

"It doesn't feel that way."

He held up the book. "I mean. Really. You wrote a book, found an agent, and got it published. And now it's a bestseller. That's not being a fraud. That's allowing God to work through you."

"I wish I saw myself the way you do."

"So why are you so tired?"

"Last night I checked into a hotel in Marietta. Someone pulled the fire alarm in the middle of the night, so I didn't get a whole lot of sleep. Then when I was driving back, I had a flat tire."

His eyes widened. "Are you OK?"

"I am now, but I sort of freaked out when I saw a motorcycle. I had a memory of the monster driving into the barn on one. I could hear you telling me to leave a situation I didn't feel comfortable in. I didn't feel comfortable, so I ran to some nearby houses."

"Good for you. I wasn't sure were listening to me or not. You were so gung-ho on being able to fight back."

"Believe me as I was running, I was so thankful you kept pushing me to get stronger and to build up my endurance. I'm sure I was just being paranoid but better safe than sorry."

Hunter looked at her and said, "The smoke alarm goes off at your hotel and you have a flat tire on the same day you go to Marietta and Charleston to talk about this Sydney Bartrum."

"I'm sure that was just a coincidence."

His gaze met hers. "There's no such thing as a coincidence when it comes to a murder investigation."

41

Hunter pushed away his empty plate. "I don't want to scare you, but I don't think it's safe for you to stay here in your house, Raven."

"Please don't say that. I'm trying to get over my paranoia. You aren't helping."

"It's not paranoia when someone's really out to get you. Apparently you ruffled some feathers when you started checking into Sydney Bartum. Most likely, the same person who killed Sydney and kidnapped you."

She bit her lip, trying not to break down. "And you think the man on the motorcycle could be him.?"

He nodded. "I'm sorry. I know that's not what you want to hear, but we have to be realistic about this. The day before you were kidnapped, Sydney Bartrum falls from the roof of her apartment. She has a large amount of unexplained money in her bank account. And then you have a flat and a motorcycle stops. As I said, there's no such thing as a coincidence in a murder investigation."

"This is exactly what I didn't want to happen. I don't want all this drama. I want to live a quiet life. It's why I used Jane Doe for the book instead of my own name."

"I know, but I think you forgot something."

"What? Because between my agent and myself, we tried to think of every possibility to protect my anonymity."

"Just because you don't know his name doesn't mean he doesn't know yours."

Raven stared at Hunter, speechless. Finally, she found her voice. "I...I can't believe I didn't think about that. Of course, you're completely right. How could I have not considered that? If I'm right that he kidnapped me because Sydney contacted me, then he certainly knew who I was. And even if it's not connected to Sydney, he would still know my name. I had my ID on me."

"True. I think it's safe to assume that your kidnapping was connected to Sydney Bartrum. PTSD can warp your perception of reality."

"I'll never be safe." Tears slid down her cheeks. She thought of her dream. The monster and her, both holding that green, glowing stick. They were tied together. And always would be. "I'll never be free of him."

"Don't think that way, Raven."

"How am I supposed to think? He didn't just steal four months from me. He stole my life."

"That's not true."

"It is true. It is." She tried to stop the tears but failed.

He sat down on the picnic bench and put his arms around her.

That only made her cry more. She'd thought Hunter might be the one but now she knew the truth. She could never have a relationship or a life. She'd always be connected to the monster holding the same glowing green stick. Raven leaned against Hunter as she cried. When they subsided, his arms were still around her. It felt good—felt right, but it couldn't happen. She forced herself to move away from him. "Sorry."

He brushed her hair out of her face. "Nothing to be sorry about." He leaned close and their lips met for a sweet, precious moment.

Raven smiled as she moved away, but it was a sad smile. It wouldn't be right to allow herself to love Hunter or to let Hunter fall in love with her. They couldn't have a future together "So now what am I supposed to do? Go into hiding?"

"For now. Until we find your monster." Hunter was confident.

"We?"

"That's what I said. You're an investigative reporter, and I'm a cop. We'll make a great team. We'll find your monster together and put an end to this."

"And then what?'

"And then I'll finish that kiss." He grinned. "But only if you want."

She couldn't help but smile.

"If you were doing a story about Sydney, what would you do next?" Hunter asked.

"Well, it would be nice if we knew who transferred the money into her account. But that information is off-limits to me, so it won't help."

"And chances are she wasn't paid that way anyway. It would be too easy to trace back to him. I have a feeling the man is very smart. He probably gave her cash that couldn't be traced back to him. And he must have some good connections. That had to be how he found you in that motel. He must be monitoring your credit cards. Whoever he is."

"You can just call him the monster. That's what I call him."

"Any other ideas how to narrow the field of suspects?"

"Sydney's friend said she helped cater some big event at the Capital Building. And we know politicians love publicity, so maybe it was reported on by the paper. Let me get my laptop." She set it up on her kitchen table and typed into the search engine.

Charleston, West Virginia political events.

"Do you know the date?"

"Good idea. She thought it was the Tuesday before Halloween, but I'll just put in October and see what happens." She typed it in and hit the enter button.

Hunter scooted his chair beside her as she scrolled through the choices, scanning the headlines.

"There." Hunter touched the screen. "What's that one about?"

Raven's heart raced as she read the details. "That's just a coincidence. It can't be the one we're looking for."

"I think we've already established I don't believe in coincidences. What's the date?"

"The Tuesday before Halloween."

"I know it sounds impossible, but the timeline works. You said her sister stated she quit her job after Thanksgiving, right?"

"Right. Senator Charles Whitman hosted a fundraiser at the West Virginia State Capital last…" She stopped reading and stood up. "I can't believe this. It has to be a mistake. There's no way the probable next President of the United States is a rapist, a kidnapper, and a murderer."

"It sounds ridiculous, but on the other hand. His

face was the first face you saw, right?"

"I didn't tell you this but when I was in West Virginia the first time I went to his house. He has a beautiful house and an amazing barn. But it wasn't the barn I was held in. Even if my memory's not completely clear I know that much."

"But you did say that he was the first man you thought was the monster. You heard his voice that night of the Presidential debates and connected it— even though you never saw his face."

She put her face in her hands and rubbed, wanting all of it to go away. "I suppose that's possible. But there's no way to prove it. And I'm absolutely sure I wasn't in his barn."

"True, but that doesn't mean he doesn't have other barns."

"This is horrible. There isn't a paper in the country that would print my allegations. I don't have a shred of proof. I don't even know if I believe it myself."

"Then that's the first step."

"What is?"

"For you to decide if Charles Whitman is your monster."

"That makes sense."

Hunter met her gaze. "And if he is, then we have to find a way to prove it. We can't let him be elected as president. Can you imagine a man that evil being president?"

"That would be horrible. A disaster."

"You can't stay here. It's not safe—no matter who the monster is. Do you want to stay with me?"

That was exactly what she wanted to do. But it wasn't the best place for her. She was too vulnerable. She didn't trust herself to stay with him. It would only make her feelings grow stronger. And at this point there was no future for them. "How about Gracie's?"

"Mmm. That's a good choice. I think. There's no real connection between the two of you. Other than she worked at your rehab center. The monster might look for you at your sister's but no reason to look at Gracie. Do you want to call her?"

She shook her head. "No phone calls. If he can monitor my credit cards, he can probably tap my phone. I'll just explain to her when I get there. Let me pack a few things."

"And leave your phone here."

"What about Amanda? She starts to panic when she can't get hold of me."

"I'll take care of that later. Right now, let's get you somewhere safe."

42

"Why are we driving this way? It's not the way to the Rehab Center."

"Just making sure no one's following us."

She hadn't thought of that. Her world suddenly became a lot scarier. What had she done to deserve all this? Was the monster right about her ruining the country by telling lies? She'd always thought she was a truth teller. But did she ruin other people's lives?

"You're awfully quiet?"

"Just thinking. Is anyone following us?"

"Not that I can tell. We'll take a few more twists and turns, and then head to Gracie's. Do you know which building she lives in?"

"Yes. I've been there a few times."

When they arrived at the Rehab Center, she directed him to Gracie's building. Once inside, they took an elevator to the third floor and then walked down the hall. She stopped walking in front of a door. "This is it. I hope she's home."

Hunter pressed the buzzer.

They waited.

"Maybe she's not home." He suggested.

"Or maybe it just takes her some time to get to the door."

His face turned red. "Yeah, you're right. I don't even think about the fact she's in a wheelchair."

"I know—"

The door opened.

"Two of my favorite people. What a nice surprise." Gracie stood in the doorway. "Come on in."

"You may not think that after we tell you why we're here," Raven said.

Gracie hobbled back to a chair and then fell into it. "I'm sure that's not true."

"You don't use your chair here?" Hunter asked.

"Not very often. The place has wheelchair accommodations, but I try to walk as much as possible. I believe the more you do, the more you can do, and the less you do the less you can do."

"I couldn't agree more with you. That's exactly what I tell my students all the time."

Gracie smiled at him. "Go ahead, you can ask me."

"Ask you what?"

"Whatever question I see in your eyes." She motioned for them to sit down. "If you'd like something to drink, the refrigerator's out there. So, what's the question?"

"It's not really my business."

"Friends share things with friends. Otherwise they're just acquaintances."

Her words brought on a fresh stab of guilt for Raven. Why was it so hard to tell people what was going on in her life? Had she always been secretive or was it her journalistic tendencies coming out?

Hunter glanced at her but smiled as if to say don't worry about it. He turned back to Gracie. "OK. If you can walk, why do you use a wheelchair?"

"So many people aren't brave enough to ask. You

know I have Neurofibromatosis Type 2. It's bad enough that it messed up my balance, but I also have several tumors on my spine that cause me pain. So between the pain and the balance issues, I wouldn't be going much of anywhere on a regular basis without the chair. With the chair I can live life on my terms."

"Got it. I hope I didn't embarrass you by asking."

"It takes a lot more than that to embarrass me, Hunter. So what's up and why are you carrying a satchel, Raven?"

"I was hoping to spend a few days with you. If you don't mind."

"I don't mind at all but what's going on?"

They'd decided to tell Gracie the only part of the story that could be verified. They didn't want to impugn anyone's name without more proof. I...uh...had a bad experience this morning. It's a long story but the gist is that I had a flat tire on the highway and thought someone might...might have done it on purpose. It sort of freaked me out."

"Oh my gosh, that's awful. Are you OK?"

"I'm fine, but I was sure glad that Hunter's been making me run as part of my training. As soon as my senses started tingling, I ran away from the car and the highway."

Gracie looked at Hunter. "And you don't want her staying at her house alone just to be on the safe side?"

He nodded. "At least for a few days."

"Of course you can stay for as long as you want."

"Thanks. It was scary."

"Good. That's settled." Hunter stood. "I'm out of here. I'll see both of you later."

43

Raven drove past her house but didn't pull into the drive. It would be ridiculous to think the monster was there, but she was afraid to go in. She'd forgotten her laptop in the rush to leave. She needed it to continue her research. For safety, she'd told Gracie where she was going and why. The trip had now turned into an ordeal. She couldn't seem to make herself go into that dark house.

A soft glow of a lantern light showed that Lydia was still up.

Maybe she'd stop in there for a minute. Raven didn't want her neighbor and future partner wondering why she wasn't home for the next few days. She pulled into Lydia's driveway on the opposite side of the house. Just stepping out into the dark creeped her out. She quickly made her way to Lydia's side door and knocked.

The door opened.

"There you are, Raven. I was beginning to worry about you. Have you been sick and at your sister's house?"

"Can I come in?" She felt vulnerable standing out on the porch.

"Of course. Of course. Where are my manners?"

Lydia opened the door wider. "So, have you been sick?"

"No. I need to go away for a few days, so I thought I'd better stop in to tell you. So you wouldn't worry. I didn't want you to think I've abandoned you or the bakery."

"Not at all. I know you have other things to do. I understand completely. Do you have another job? Is that what keeps you so busy?"

"I don't actually have a job right now. I used to be a reporter, and I've been doing research for an article I might write. For a newspaper."

"Oh, how exciting."

"I'm not sure if I'll actually write the article. I have to wait and see how the research turns out."

"Would you like a piece of pie?"

Raven smiled. Lydia loved to feed her. "No. I just stopped in to let you know what was going on with me. I probably won't be around for the next few days. But if anyone comes to the house looking for me, please don't tell them anything."

"Of course not. Your business is yours alone. Let me get some pie before you go. Sit. Sit. It won't take but a minute."

Raven sat.

Lydia walked back in with a huge piece chocolate cream pie.

"That looks amazing."

"It's a sin to brag, but yes, it does taste pretty good."

Raven took a bite. "Wow. It's even better than it looks. You'll have to teach me how to make it."

"I can do that." Lydia smiled. "So if you're staying somewhere else, why are you here?"

"I forgot my laptop."

"That is your computer?"

She nodded since her mouth was full of the rich chocolate concoction.

"But you certainly must need that for your work."

She swallowed. "I do. But you know how I'm afraid of the dark. I don't want to go in my house. I'll come back to get it tomorrow. When it's light."

"Nonsense. You eat the pie, and I'll get it. I'm not afraid of the dark. We Amish spend a lot of time in the dark." She walked over with an outstretched hand. "Keys."

"You don't have to do that."

"Of course I don't have to. I want to." She held out her hand.

Raven handed her the keys.

"I'll be right back."

"It's on the kitchen table. You have to unplug it and bring the cord, too."

"OK."

Raven stuffed the last of the pie in her mouth, feeling ashamed. She was a grown woman. She should have got the laptop herself. But Hunter and Gracie both said it wasn't wrong to ask for help. She felt ridiculous sitting here while Lydia went into her own house for her. Really, if it was dangerous for me, wasn't it just as dangerous for Lydia? The thought made her heart thump. Of course it was. She stood up.

A scream split the quiet neighborhood.

And then a gunshot.

Raven ran out the door and down Lydia's porch.

A shadow was running up her steps. The shadow turned. "Go back in the house." Hunter's voice was rough.

"Lydia's in there."

"I know. I'll check on her." He moved toward the door.

She hesitated and then ran toward her house.

Lydia was on the floor in a pool of blood.

"Call 911." Hunter yelled. "She's been shot."

44

"This is all my fault." Raven's tears had dried, but her heart was still wobbly with guilt.

They were sitting in the waiting room of the emergency room.

The ambulance and the police cars had left the ER entrance, leaving two officers to guard the OR while Lydia was in surgery. Later, they'd accompany her to her hospital room. Between the sheriff, Hunter, and the deputies, they'd decided to treat Lydia as a witness until the case was over.

Hunter held her hand. "It's nobody's fault except the man who shot her, Raven."

"How can you say it's not my fault? She went in there for me. Because I forgot my laptop and I was too afraid to go in myself. It's all my fault." She stopped talking and looked at him. "Why were you even at my house?"

"I was doing a stakeout. Waiting to see if you had any uninvited visitors. I saw you pull into Lydia's and then go in her house."

"I didn't see you."

"That's the idea. Watch the person or place without them knowing about it."

"So you didn't see anyone go in my house?"

"Nope. I guess I should have had someone watching the back of the house. But it wasn't official. I was doing it on my own."

"Do you think it was him?" She lowered her voice. "Charles Whitman."

"I don't know who it was but I'm sure it had something to do with your monster—whoever he is. It might not have been him personally in your house. A man like that can pay for goons to do his dirty work."

The doctor walked out. His green scrubs were covered with blood.

The world started turning wavy. Please, God. Give me your peace. Raven focused on the doctor. The world came back into view.

"Are you here for Lydia?" At Hunter's nod, he continued, "She'll be fine. She got shot in the shoulder. But she hit her head when she fell. That's where most of the blood was from. We'll keep her in the hospital for a few days because of the concussion, but there's no reason to think that she won't have a full recovery."

Raven breathed a sigh of relief. "Oh, thank God, she's going to be all right."

"She's in recovery now. You won't be able to talk with her for a few more hours." He held up a small baggie. "Here's the bullet. I know all about chain of custody. I signed and dated it. And now it's your responsibility." He handed the bag to Hunter and walked back through the swinging doors.

Hunter pulled out his cell phone and updated the sheriff about Lydia's condition. When he hung up, he looked at her. "The sheriff needs to question both of us."

"What should I say to him?"

"Tell him the truth. About what happened tonight

and last night as well. Not about our theories. Since we don't have any proof, I don't think it will help to share those right now."

"Makes sense." She nodded. "I can't believe this. It's like a nightmare only I'm awake."

"We'll let the sheriff's investigation go wherever it goes. If it leads to your monster, so much the better. If it doesn't, then it doesn't. We'll have to wait to see what happens."

She nodded. "Do you think it's safe for me to go back to Gracie's?"

"I think so. But again, we need to take some precautions to make sure you're not being followed before you go back to her apartment."

45

"I don't see how I can stay at Gracie's without telling her the truth. All of it. I can't put anyone else in danger. I probably shouldn't even come back here in the first place."

Hunter and Raven walked down the hall toward Gracie's apartment hand in hand.

"I agree, but I don't believe either of you are in danger as long as you stay here, and nobody knows where you are. If I thought that I wouldn't have brought you here."

Raven hit the buzzer but slid the key card in. As she opened the door, she called, "It's just me, Gracie."

Grace sat in a chair with a book in her hand. "Good thing, I've been worried. You've been gone for hours. I thought you'd be gone thirty or forty minutes." She noticed Hunter. "So that's what's been keeping you busy."

"It's not like that, Gracie." Hunter walked in. "We need to talk to you and it's serious."

Gracie nodded. "I can see that by the blood on both of you. What happened? Were you in an accident?"

"Not exactly. My neighbor, Lydia got shot."

"Your neighbor got shot? And you were there?"

"Actually she got shot in my house. I was in her house at the time. And Hunter was watching my house so when we heard the shot, we both ran in and found Lydia."

Gracie looked at Raven then at Hunter and then back at Raven. "Sit down. I'll make us some coffee. Seems like we might have a lot to discuss."

"You're right, but you sit. I'll make the coffee." Hunter spoke up. "And we'll tell you all about it. I don't want you to think we were hiding things from you before."

"Except that you were." Gracie smiled to take the edge off her words.

Raven sat down. "That's true, but after you hear the whole story, I think you'll understand why we felt like it was better not to tell everything. And really, I promise you I would never have come here if I thought it would endanger you."

"So, does that mean because you're here you don't think I'm in danger?"

"To be truthful, I'm not sure, Gracie. I'll let you be the judge of that after you hear everything. And if you want me to leave, I won't be upset. In fact, I really didn't want to come back. Hunter's the one who convinced me it would be safe."

"Let's hear it."

Hunter made coffee while Raven talked to Gracie. She started at the beginning. Her memories. Her book. Her trips to Marietta and Charleston. Their theories about Sydney's death. Raven finally ended with how Lydia got shot.

Gracie didn't say anything as she sipped coffee. She broke the silence with a question. "OK. So you've told me but you haven't told me who you think the man is. Do you have a name?"

"Charles Whitman, III."

Gracie closed her eyes for a moment then nodded. "But we discussed this, and you agreed it couldn't be him. That is was your memories playing tricks on you."

Hunter picked up the thread, telling her what made them think it was indeed Charles Whitman. "But we're also keeping an open mind. If our research leads us to a different person—so be it."

"I can't believe this. And I'm the one who convinced you it wasn't Whitman but that it was your mind filling in the blank spaces."

"And you may still be right about that. It's such an outlandish accusation, I'm not one hundred percent convinced."

"So how will you find out who it is?"

"That's why I went back to get my laptop. I wanted to listen to some of his interviews. See if his voice matched the voice I remember from the barn."

"That makes sense. And I just happen to have a smart TV. I'm sure he'll have some interviews on social media and video sites." She picked up the remote. "Anything in particular you'd like to hear him say?"

"Yes. If you can find a clip where he uses the word patriot that might be helpful."

"Coming right up."

A few moments later Charles Whitman's face filled the TV screen.

"OK, Raven." Gracie appeared worried. "I want you to close your eyes as you listen to the tape. Try to stay relaxed. I know that's easier said than done but do your best."

Raven sat back against the sofa and took several

deep breaths.

Hunter covered her hand with his.

Gracie hit the start button.

Charles Whitman's voice filled the quiet room. "I want to be President of this great country for one reason and one reason only. I'm a patriot. It's that simple. I love this country and I want it be great once again."

Raven gasped and her hand flew to her mouth. "That's...that's what he said that night I was watching the debate. It triggered my memories."

"I'll play it again. Keep an open mind and just listen."

Raven listened once more and then opened his eyes.

Gracie and Hunter were staring at her.

"It's him. That's the voice in the barn."

"Are you absolutely sure?"

"It wasn't just his voice. He actually said those exact words to me. About being a patriot and that I was just a liar reporter trying to ruin the country."

"He had my vote. We have to stop him. Now. Before the election. We can't let him become president." Gracie shuddered. "The thought of someone that evil being president is terrifying."

Raven looked at Gracie. "You believe me?"

"Of course I believe you."

"Just like that? No doubts. No thinking it's my imagination or my brain just filling in the blank spots."

Gracie shook her head. "Do you have any doubts?"

"No."

"Then neither do I." She looked at Hunter. "What about you?"

"If Raven says he's the monster, then he's the monster. The question is how will we prove it?"

"And prove it before the election." Gracie added.

"First we have to find the barn he kept me in."

"That means a title search. Easy peasy." Gracie grabbed her keyboard. "I think we can assume it was in West Virginia since that was where you were found and that's where he's from."

"I'm not sure about that. I've looked at maps of the area. West Virginia, Maryland, and Virginia all come together there in that area."

"True but you floated downstream and that most likely means West Virginia." Hunter looked up from his phone where he'd already brought up a map of the area.

"I guess you're probably right about that."

Gracie maneuvered through site after site until she ended up at the land title office of West Virginia. She looked at them. "OK. This is it." She typed in Charles Whitman III.

They all watched the screen.

"This shows that he owns three separate holdings, but it looks as if they're all adjacent to each other. And all in Morgan County. Looks like he's owned two of them for a long time and the third he purchased three years ago."

"I've been to his house." She met Gracie's gaze. "When I went down to Berkeley Springs, I sort of ended up at his house. Much closer to a mansion. I already told Hunter that I even saw the barn. It was brand new and immaculate and not the place I was kept."

"Of course, that doesn't mean there couldn't be another barn on the property."

"Except his caretaker told me they tore down his old barn to build the new one. Plus, he has several employees who work there. I can't believe they'd all be in on him keeping a kidnapped woman."

"Could he own other properties that his name's not connected to?" Hunter asked.

"Sure, they could be owned by his companies or even other family members."

"Let me see if I can find out anything about his family." Hunter went to a search engine. "He has a sister. Her name is Bethany Whitman-Franks. Can you do a property search for her? It looks as if she doesn't live in the area any longer because she lives in New York with her husband."

"I certainly can." A moment later. "I'm not seeing anything. Oh, wait...here's something. It seems she donated some piece of property to Morgan County a few months ago. I can't find anything else about it."

"It's amazing how much one can find out about anyone else with just a few clicks of the keyboard," Raven said. "I doubt that he'd let his sister donate property to the county if it was where I was held."

They spent the next hour trying to figure out a way to prove that Charles Whitman was her monster.

Finally, Hunter stood. "Enough. This isn't getting us anywhere. Let's all go to sleep and maybe one of us will have an idea tomorrow."

46

Charles Whitman was furious. How did this woman keep getting away from him? He would not let this little nobody ruin his chance to be President. It was his right and his destiny. He pounded a fist on the sofa arm. He couldn't believe it when that little Amish woman had walked into Suzie Q's house. He didn't know who was more surprised. It was a good thing she hadn't turned on the light. She'd noticed him just as he'd pulled the trigger, but it had been dark. He didn't think she could identify him.

Blunders and more blunders.

It was all getting away from him.

He had to put a stop to it now otherwise he'd lose his presidency before it even began.

There was a knock on his hotel door.

They were in Cleveland at the moment, but tomorrow the plan was to make it to every major city in Ohio. After all, as Ohio voted so did the nation. With only a week left before the primary, it was important to get Ohio behind him. "Come in."

His assistant walked in. "I hate to bother you, sir."

"What do you need, Robert?"

"It's not what I need, sir. It's what do you need? I know something's wrong. I've known you too long to not be able to tell that."

"I won't insult your intelligence by denying it but it's my problem. I'll work it out."

"Sir, it's your job to get elected President. It's my job to take care of you. Just tell me what you need done and I'll do it."

They're gazes met.

"Anything, sir. I believe in you. I want you to be the next President of the United States."

"Thank you for your vote of confidence, Robert, but this is something I need to handle on my own."

"Begging your pardon, sir. No, it's not. I'm your man. I'll get it done. I'll take care of the small annoyances so you can focus on the big picture. You tell me the problem and I'll take care of it."

Charles Whitman stared at his long-time assistant. "Anything, Robert?"

Without blinking, he said, "Anything, sir."

"It is a small annoyance but it could become a big headache for me. Remember I had you look into that reporter?"

"Raven Marks. Yes, sir, I remember the name well."

"Turns out she lives in a small town south of here. I think she's become obsessed with me. And she's threatened to make up lies about me if I won't hire her. Those lies could ruin me."

"We can't have that, sir."

"The thing is I've deleted all my correspondence with her that would prove she's threatening me. If I had some emails and such that would prove she's trying to blackmail me, it would make things much easier."

Without a blink, Robert nodded. "Not a problem,

sir. One of my degrees is computer science. By the time you wake up in the morning, you'll find all sorts of threats she's made to you over the course of the last few months. You can show them to the Secret Service if that's the way you want it handled. Or I can find a more expedient way to handle her. After all, I was Special Forces. If you want. Your choice."

Charles understood the unspoken offer. "I think letting the Secret Service take care of the matter would be fine." He would discredit her before she could discredit him.

47

"What do you mean the Secret Service was at your house?" Raven's voice squeaked. She was on Hunter's phone talking to Amanda.

Amanda answered, "Just what I said. They wanted to know where you were. Said you weren't at your house. When I told them I didn't know they asked to come in to check."

"Did you let them? Did they have a warrant?"

"They didn't show me one if they had it, but, of course, I let them in. It's not like you were here. Where are you? What's going on?"

"Better that you don't know. That way you don't have to lie to them. If they come to your house again, just tell them the truth. I called you but wouldn't tell you where I was. What did you tell them?"

"What could I say? I gave them your address, but they said they'd already been there and that you weren't there. And they said, there'd been a shooting at your house last night. Is that true?"

They knew about that? What else did they know? Raven stared at the cell phone in her hand. "I can't talk to you right now, Amanda. I have to hang up and don't worry about me, but I won't be able to call you for the next few days."

"What's going on, Raven?"

"I don't know, but I'm safe. And you need to stay safe. You cooperate with them in any way they need. I haven't done anything wrong. No matter what they tell you. And trust Hunter." As soon as she broke the connection, she began breaking down Hunter's cell phone.

Gracie walked in. "What are you doing?"

"It's probably too late but I'm trying to keep the Secret Service from finding my location." She took the battery out.

"The Secret Service?"

"They were just at Amanda's house. They wanted to know where I was."

"Did she tell them?"

"She didn't know so she couldn't tell them. I sort of hung up on her." She picked up the battery. "They might have already traced my phone. Of course it's Hunter's phone, so I think that it's OK. But who knows? Do you think they could do that? So quickly?"

"I have no idea. I'm a counselor not a cop."

"Speaking of cops, maybe I should call Hunter." Raven looked at Gracie. "Maybe not. I don't want to get him in trouble."

"Don't they need some kind of court order before they can monitor phone calls?"

"I think so, but that's the regular police. I have no idea what kind of power the Secret Service may have. Maybe they don't have to follow the same rules. In the name of national security."

"Why do you think they even want to talk to you?"

"Because of Charles Whitman. I guess. But certainly he wouldn't give them my name? Not if he's done the things we think he's done."

"Doesn't make sense to me either." Gracie's phone rang. She picked it up. "It's the main office." She pushed a button so the call would be on speaker. "Hello."

"Gracie, I've got the Secret Service in my office. They're looking for Raven Marks. Do you happen to know where she is?"

Gracie motioned for Raven to leave the room.

Raven ran out.

"Not really. Probably at her house at this time of the morning."

Raven smiled as she listened from her spot in Gracie's bedroom. Technically true since Gracie couldn't see her. She might be in the bathroom or the kitchen.

"I told them the two of you were friends. They want to talk to you."

"About what?"

"They didn't say. Only that it was about national security."

"I can get there in about ten minutes or so."

"OK, they'll be waiting."

Gracie hung up. "Did you hear all that?"

Raven walked back out. "This is crazy. I haven't done anything that should concern national security or the Secret Service."

"That may be, but what better way to stop you from exposing him than by discrediting you?"

"That makes a lot of sense. I guess I was right about who my monster is."

"I'm so sorry I talked you out of believing it. It's just seemed…" She shrugged.

"Unbelievable. Impossible. I know. What do you

think I should I do now, Gracie?"

"I think you probably need to leave. Who knows, they might ask to search my apartment. If they do, I might not have time to warn you."

"I don't even have a car."

"You can take mine. The keys are on the counter."

"But—"

"Just take them and go. And take my phone with you. I'll call you later. If I think it's safe."

"OK."

"I'm heading over to my office. Better take your things with you. Just in case they do check my apartment. I wouldn't want them to find your stuff here. That might be hard to explain."

As soon as Gracie left, a part of her wanted to break down. To give up. Hadn't she been through enough because of this monster? God, I trust you.

She took a deep breath. She didn't have time for a pity party. She hurried to the bedroom, stuffed her things in the satchel, and grabbed the keys. As she opened the door, she heard voices in the hall.

She closed the door but left it open enough to hear.

"Ma'am, we'd like to check your apartment if you don't mind?"

"But I do mind. That's an invasion of my privacy."

"If you don't have anything to hide there shouldn't be a problem."

Panic rose up in Raven. This was the only door in the apartment. Gracie wouldn't be able to stop them for long.

"I don't have anything to hide but I believe in due process. You know, I'm a counselor so I know all about due process. So, let me see your warrant." She was stalling for time.

"Is that how you're really playing this?"

"I believe in—"

"Due process. Yeah, I heard that. OK, we don't have a warrant to search your apartment, but we do have an arrest warrant for Raven Marks. If we have reason to believe she's in your apartment, we have a right to enter. How's that for due process, ma'am?"

Raven had heard enough, she had to get out of here. She ran to the sliding window, unlocked it, and went out on the small balcony. The second floor. She stared down. How bad could it be? She'd been tossed from a cliff, so this was easy, right?

Raven tossed over the satchel, then climbed on the railing. Keep me safe, God. She took a deep breath and then climbed down still holding on to the railing. When she ran out of railing, she let go. Fortunately, she landed on her side instead of her legs. She jumped up.

With no idea where she should go or what she should do, she ran to Gracie's car.

48

A warrant for her arrest? The words kept spinning around Raven's head as she kept driving the back roads of Holmes County, not sure where to go. It felt surreal, like a dream. Or more like a nightmare. A truly horrifying nightmare. All she'd wanted was justice. But now she was the one being hunted.

And even worse, Gracie might be in trouble because of her. At least Raven hadn't been there when the men came in. Because it sounded like Gracie was losing that battle when she'd jumped off the balcony.

The only problem was that she'd forgotten to shut the sliding door before she jumped. But at least they hadn't found her in the apartment. But she couldn't keep driving Gracie's car. If they found her in it, Gracie could be in trouble and that was the last thing Raven wanted.

Time to start making some decisions.

She drove Gracie's car to the Akron Canton Airport, took the battery out of the cell phone Gracie had given her, and then left that in the car as well. Just in case they were tracking Gracie's phone.

Then she walked inside to rent a car but realized she'd need her credit card. That would lead them right back to her. This wouldn't work. She sat down in a chair to think.

Maybe she should just fly somewhere. But she'd need her credit card and ID for that as well. If they really had an arrest warrant for her, that probably wouldn't work either. Right now, she needed to find a place to rest and regroup. There had to be a way out of this mess, but she needed time to figure out what it was.

And then it came to her. A bus. Busses didn't require IDs, only a ticket. She'd get a taxi and head to the bus station, but first she needed cash. A lot of it. She looked around for an ATM machine. She slipped her card in and held her breath, praying that her account hadn't been frozen. As the money slid out, she breathed a sigh of relief then walked outside.

Two hours later, Raven saw the sign that said, 'Welcome to Pennsylvania' from her bus seat. As the bus pulled into the station, she grabbed her satchel and walked away, feeling only slightly safer. She went outside. Her gaze landed on a motel across the road.

She walked into the small establishment. "I need a room."

The clerk handed her the registration slip without even looking at her. "Fill this out."

Raven stared at it. The last time she'd done that things hadn't turned out well. "Look. The truth is I don't want anyone to know I'm here. Can I just pay you in cash and you not put me in the system?"

He barely blinked. "Double the price. That's the going rate for love in the afternoon."

Her cheeks burned with embarrassment. "Fine. How much is that?"

"Let's just make it an even two hundred."

Good thing she'd gone the ATM earlier. "How

about one fifty?"

"Two hundred."

She wasn't in a position to barter. She reached in her purse and handed him two one-hundred-dollar bills. She put her hand out and he gave her the key card.

He smirked. "Have a good time."

She left without answering him. The room was just what she expected. Nothing grand but it was clean enough. She needed to make phone calls. She stared at the phone in the room. The only phone she had at the moment.

Would the government be monitoring Gracie's and Hunter's home phones? She really had no idea. On the other hand, she had a warrant out for her arrest for threatening a presidential candidate. That was probably serious enough to warrant government intrusion—even if it was a false accusation.

She couldn't take a chance on them tracing her to this motel in Pennsylvania. She walked outside and looked around the area. A small strip mall was next to the motel. Maybe they'd have a phone store.

And they did.

Twenty minutes later she walked back into her motel room with two prepaid phones. The clerk at the store helped her activate it without using her credit cards or name. It had been easier than expected. She'd ended up buying two after the clerk explained that the phone could be tracked if someone found out her number.

Her plan was to call Gracie, and then Hunter with one phone. And then she'd use the second phone if she needed to contact them again. She hoped that the two different numbers would throw them off her track.

She sat down on the bed, finally able to breathe. What a mess. The thought of Hunter made her start to cry. When she finished, she felt better. *God is with me.* She could handle this—or anything else the monster threw at her. She wouldn't let him ruin her life a second time. This time she would win. She couldn't let the monster become President.

She searched for the number of the Rehab Center then dialed it.

The main switchboard answered.

"I need Grace's office."

"One moment."

A second later the phone rang.

"Hello."

"Don't say my name just tell me what's going on."

"Where are you? I've been sitting here praying for you," Grace said.

"It's better if you don't know where I am. That way you won't have to lie for me. I'm so sorry for bringing you into this."

"Don't think that way. This isn't your fault. All I'm doing is helping a friend."

Tears filled Raven's eyes. "Thank you."

"You don't have to thank me. They claim they have a bunch of emails from you to the senator threatening him."

"I never emailed him. Ever."

"They say you did."

"Do you believe them?"

"Of course not."

"Have you talked to, you know, my other friend?"

"He wants you to call him at his office. On the office line. He said he'd wait there until you call him."

"OK. Your car is at the Akron airport."

"Not a problem. I'll get it later. Did you jump off the balcony?"

"It was the only way to get out, so I did."

"Are you hurt?"

"Just a little sore. Did they notice the open door?"

"They did. They walked out of it, but I guess you were gone by then. Thankfully. What are you going to do?"

"I have no idea."

"I'll be praying for you."

"Please do." Raven hung up and did a web search for the Holmes County Sheriff Department but didn't hit the icon to dial. She had to think about this. If she called, Hunter would want to come. And if he did that, it could ruin his career. On the other hand, he'd said they were partners and they would figure this out together

The Bible said if anyone wanted wisdom all they had to do was ask for it. *God, I need Your wisdom. There has to be a way to stop this monster, but I don't know what it is. Show me. Show me the way.* She laid back on the bed and forced her breathing to slow. One breath. *God give me Your wisdom.* Another breath. *God give me Your wisdom.* A third breath…

Raven opened her eyes. She couldn't believe she'd actually fallen asleep. Her watch showed her it hadn't been a long nap but it was enough. But she had a plan. *Thank You, God.*

The plan wasn't about getting evidence. Hopefully that evidence could be found later. Or not. This wasn't about court, it was about stopping a monster from becoming the President. She only needed to convict Charles Whitman, III in the court of popular opinion. That was the only thing that mattered.

49

Raven stared out the window of her motel room in the early morning hours. Not quite dawn but not night either. She prayed this day would be easier than the previous one.

She smiled when she saw Hunter's truck drive in and walked out to greet him. They clung to each other for a few moments.

"Are you sure you're OK?" Hunter asked.

"I'm fine. Are you sure nobody followed you?"

"Yes, but we should get out of here just the same. We can talk in the truck."

"Good idea."

Once they were both in the truck, he asked, "Where are we going?"

"You got a GPS?"

He pointed at the built-in one on his dash. She typed in the address. "It's all set. Just follow the instructions."

He looked at the location she'd punched in. "New York City?"

"New York City."

"Why?"

"I'll tell you all about it but let me explain everything before you tell me what a horrible idea it is."

"Apparently, I'm not going to like it, huh?"

"Probably not. But it wasn't my idea."

"Really? Whose is it?"

"God's. So you see, you can't really argue with God. He always knows best."

"And exactly how did God tell you His idea?"

"Well, He didn't actually tell me. But I prayed and prayed for wisdom. Then I fell asleep. When I woke up I had this idea."

"And that's why you're blaming God?"

"I'm not blaming God. I happen to think it's a great idea. And I think you will, too."

"OK, let's hear this great idea?"

"At this point, we have to forget about getting evidence to prove what he did to me in a court of law. The only court we need to worry about is the court of popular opinion. We can't let him become President. Right now, we have to tell people what he did to me. What he did to Sydney Bartrum, and probably other women, as well. We have to stop them from voting for him."

"I see what you're saying. So you're giving up on making sure he gets prosecuted for what he did to you? And to Sydney Bartrum?"

"Not giving up, just postponing it." She shrugged. "But the truth is we may never get enough evidence to convict him of his crimes. But I'll do everything I can to make sure he never becomes President."

"And that will be enough for you?"

"For now?"

"You may end up being the one to get convicted. The Secret Service is working hard to prove you're the dangerous one. If you forget about all this, they may forget all about you as well. And you can just live the quiet life you want."

"I can't do that."

"Why not?"

She grinned. "Because I'm a patriot."

"Not funny."

"I sort of thought it was. And it's not a joke. I don't want that monster to be president of anything, let alone my country."

"I'm just telling you it's not too late to change your mind."

"My mind is made up."

50

"Of all people, why would you pick the one woman who was outright rude to you while she interviewed you?" Hunter was maneuvering through the streets of Brooklyn.

"Because of that. I didn't want to go to the fluffy reporters. This is a real story, and Shanley DeForest has more reach and influence than the others."

"I suppose that's true. But I'm surprised she even agreed to meet with you."

Raven wasn't looking forward to seeing Shanley DeForest again. "I promised to reveal my name and all the other details, plus an exclusive about my recovered memories. She couldn't resist."

"Why not just meet her at the TV station?"

"I'm not sure. It just didn't feel like the right thing to do. I guess I just didn't want to deal with all the people there." Raven's one condition had been that she wouldn't come to the station for the interview. Instead, they were meeting at some house in Brooklyn.

Hunter slowed down and then pulled into a drive. "This is it."

A moment later the garage door opened. A man walked out. "Hey, Shanley will be here any time. She's notorious for being late. By the way, I'm Ron."

"Not a problem." Hunter shook hands. "I'm Hunter."

"I'm Raven Marks, better known as Jane Doe."

"I was the cameraman on the first interview. I like your real hair better than that red, curly mop."

"Really? I sort of liked that look."

"Stick with your natural hair."

"Thanks."

He pointed at a table. "There's some coffee or juice over there. I made a few sandwiches. Well, my wife did. I thought you might be hungry."

"Actually, I am." Raven walked over and chose a ham and cheese.

Hunter did the same.

"Help yourself, I'll go call Shanley to see where she is." Ron walked into his house.

Raven looked around. Ron had set up a background screen and two chairs. Apparently, that's where the magic would take place. She only hoped this would work out the way she planned.

A car pulled in behind theirs. Shanley stepped out.

Raven felt frumpy compared to her. Maybe she should have dressed up a little more. Oh, well, it wasn't easy to be glamorous when one was on the run from the Secret Service.

Shanley walked up. "No wig this time, huh?"

"I promised I'd reveal my name and what I've remembered so no need to disguise myself."

"So you've remembered what happened to you."

"In excruciating detail."

"Tell me about it, and then I'll know what to ask on camera."

Raven shook her head. "Let's just do it all on camera. You ask what you want, and I'll give as honest answers as I can."

Shanley squinted at her. "That's not the way I want to do it."

Raven met her gaze. "It's the only way I'll do it."

"Why?"

"Because some of the things I'll tell you will be quite shocking. If I tell you now, you won't be surprised. And your viewers will be able to tell that."

Ron walked out. "There you are, Shan. I called but you didn't answer. Are you ready?"

"I suppose so." She walked over and took a seat. "Make sure you get a lot of close ups of our...can I at least know your name?"

"Raven Marks."

"Make sure you get a lot of close ups of Raven's face. Let the viewers see the real Jane Doe."

"Will do."

Raven walked over and sat down. She closed her eyes, praying for the right words and the ability to stay calm through this ordeal. When she opened then, Hunter gave her a thumbs-up.

Shanley smirked. "Praying?"

Raven sat up straighter. "Yes. I'm ready."

Shanley made a motion to Ron. "I'm Shanley DeForest, and you're watching a very special edition of A View of the World. As you can see, we're not in the studio today. We took a field trip to an undisclosed location to talk with my special guest. Raven Marks. How are you today, Raven?"

"I'm happy to be here."

"Now you probably don't recognize Raven, but she's the bestselling author of *Unsinkable* by Jane Doe. That's right, folks, you're looking at the real Jane Doe. Why did you decide to reveal your real identity,

Raven?"

"I didn't have a choice. I've remembered most of what happened to me during my disappearance. People need to know what happened and who kidnapped me."

Shanley's eyes widened. "Are you telling me you know who kidnapped you?"

"That's what I'm telling you."

"Have the police arrested him?"

"No."

"Why not?"

"Because I haven't told them."

"Why not?"

"Because I don't have any proof, Shanley. I only have my memories, and any attorney could poke lots of holes in that, considering my medical history."

"Then why come forward at all? Why not go to the police with your…accusations and let them get the proof? That's their job."

"I will do exactly that. After this interview. But the world needs to know the name of the man who kidnapped me. Actually, not the world, just Americans. We have an election coming up, and they need to be fully informed about their choices."

Shanley started to speak and then stopped as if gathering her thoughts. "Are you telling me this person has something to do with the upcoming elections?"

Raven took a deep breath and met Shanley's gaze. "That's exactly what I'm telling you."

"Tell us who your monster is. Yes, I read your book."

"Before I do that, I want to tell you what lead up to me being kidnapped. I do have that proof. I was contacted by a woman name Sydney Bartrum. She wanted me to do a story about something that happened to her. Before we could meet, she died."

"Murdered?"

"The official cause says accidental death, but, yes, I believe she was murdered. She died on May fourth in Columbus, Ohio. I was kidnapped on May fifth from the Welcome Center in West Virginia across the river from Marietta, Ohio, where I worked as a reporter. I don't believe the timing is a coincidence."

"I must say this story is quite compelling. And you're saying you do have proof that she contacted you."

"I do. But it's a good thing I printed it out because someone has now wiped away my entire cloud."

"And you think she was killed because she contacted you?"

"She told me she had a secret. And when she was going to come forward with it, she was killed. And then I was kidnapped and was supposed to die, but God intervened. He saved me for a reason. This reason. To not let the monster become President."

Shanley stared as if speechless. Finally, she asked, "Who kidnapped you?"

Raven took a deep breath and looked directly into the camera. "Charles Whitman the Third."

Shanley stared at Raven for a moment then made a slashing motion across her neck. "Stop filming, Ron. Stop right now. I can't use this any of this."

"Why not? It's the truth," Hunter said.

Shanley stood up. "I don't know if it's true or not. This could be some elaborate ruse to get your candidate elected. I can't be a party to something like this without proof. Do you have any proof?" She demanded. "If you can show me proof, maybe I can get the station to run this. Without proof, no way."

"I have the copy of the email that Sydney sent me. Her sister can verify that she had almost a hundred thousand dollars in her bank account, and no way to account for that kind of money."

"Can you show that Whitman was the one who gave her the money?"

"Not yet. I don't have those kinds of connections. The police will have to do that. But I'm willing to take a lie detector test to prove I'm telling the truth. I know he's the man who kidnapped me because I remember him."

"A lie detector test isn't admissible in court."

"This isn't about court. It's about making sure that monster isn't elected President. That's what this is about."

"I'm sorry. I...I just can't believe this. I've met Senator Whitman several times. He seems like an honorable man. A good man. I refuse to be used by some personal agenda you have to nail Whitman as this horrible..."

Nail. Raven's world turned wavy. And she was back in the barn. Chained. But she had a nail in her hand. She was standing on her tiptoes. Using the nail she'd scratched on a wooden window sill. *R-A* –she kept scratching— <u>V-E-N</u>. She kept scratching. Her name. The year. Then she was spitting in her hand. Rubbing it in her name. More spitting. More rubbing. The world came back into view.

Hunter's arms were around her.

Shanley and Ron were staring at her.

Ron asked, "Are you OK? What happened?"

"I...I just had a memory."

"What was it?" Shanley asked.

"Will you broadcast this? It's all the truth."

"I'm sorry. I just can't. Not without proof. I refuse to ruin a good man because of…" She shook her head. "I just don't believe it."

Should she tell Shanley what she'd remembered? It would be proof she needed. But only if she could find the barn where she'd been chained up. Before Charles could destroy the proof that she'd been in that place. "Just remember, you could have broken the story. And didn't."

"I won't be a party to an unsubstantiated witch hunt. You've wasted enough of my time." Shanley looked at Ron. "Destroy that film. I won't be a party to some sort of vendetta against a good man." She walked toward her car.

Raven followed, yelling, desperate to convince her. "He's not a good man. He's a monster. He kidnapped me and tortured me. Then he threw me off a cliff. He killed Sydney Bartrum. That's who Charles Whitman is."

Shanley stopped and turned back. "I don't believe any of it. Someone's paying you to make these horrible accusations." She got in her car and drove away.

Hunter walked up to her and hugged her. "It's OK. You did your best. We'll think of another way."

Before she could answer, Ron walked up. "Raven, I believe you. I'll make sure this gets out on the Internet. I'll edit out Shanley's face and just use her voice without identifying her. I can disguise the voice so the public won't know it's her. She won't like it, but there won't be a whole lot she can do about it. Especially after I get it on the Internet."

She moved out of Hunter's hug. "You believe me?

You believe he did those things?"

"I do." He seemed to consider something. "I've met Whitman. I thought...well, I thought there was something off about him for a long time. I just figured he was a typical greedy politician. But he always seemed to be hiding behind a façade. More so than most I've met."

"Won't you get in trouble?"

"Maybe, but I'll make so much money off of this that I won't need to work for a while. And in the end, I'll probably get a promotion. I'll be glad to split the money with you."

"I'm not doing it for the money. I just want the truth out there even if I can't prove it in a legal court. Keep the money."

Ron pointed at the camera. "OK, I have it on film telling me that."

"You kept filming?"

He nodded.

She smiled. "Good. Thank you so much. I think I may have a way to get the proof. Do you have a number I can call you if I get it?" She took a deep breath. "When I get it."

He pulled a card from his wallet and handed it to her. "Do you want me to wait for your call?"

"That's up to you. I'll let you decide that for yourself. But I'll call you either way."

Once they were in the car, Hunter looked at her. "How are you getting proof?"

"I remembered something back there, but I didn't want to tell Shanley about it since she doesn't believe me. But we have to find that barn he held me in."

"And how will we do that?"

"I think I know someone who might be able to

help."

51

Hunter and Raven walked into the building.

"Oh my. I...I can't believe you're here." Martha Borden looked up from her computer screen. Tears ran down her cheeks. "It's all over the Internet. And now the TV. All those things you're saying. About Chuck. They can't be true."

"Very true. I'm here to ask you to help me."

"I can't. Chuck is about to be elected President. He's saying you just made everything up because he wouldn't hire you. If I help you, Matt could lose his job. The people around here love Chuck. We would be pariahs in our home."

"What about you, Martha?"

She shook her head. "I...there's nothing I can do."

"That's not what I'm asking, Martha. You know I'm telling the truth, don't you? You know the real Charles Whitman. The one no one else knows."

"Nobody believes you. They're saying you're making the whole thing up. Even that Shanley lady."

"Well you know that's not true, Martha. You know I was thrown off a cliff and almost died. I spent months and months in rehab learning how to walk again. You know I was held against my will for months."

"I know you were hurt, and you were found. But

as Matt says, you could've jumped off the cliff yourself. Faked your disappearance. Then wrote that book just so you could ruin Chuck's chances of being elected. And so you can make money. Get famous. Everybody wants to be famous nowadays."

"You don't really believe that, do you, Martha?"

She shook her head and backed away from them. "I don't know what to believe. I just know you need to get out of here. If people around here realize who you are, they might hurt you. You should leave. Even Matt is infuriated with you."

"Martha. I saw something in your eyes that day. When I came in here, and we were talking about Charles Whitman. You may speak the party line like everyone else around here. About what a good guy he is. But I think you know something else about him, don't you? I think you know the evil that lives inside him."

She held up a hand as if to stop Raven's words. "I said I don't know anything."

"You can say it all you want but that won't change the reality. Will it, Martha?"

Martha's lips quivered. "It was so long ago. It doesn't matter now. And it was all my fault. I shouldn't have—"

"It wasn't your fault and it matters, Martha." Raven's voice was quiet. She hadn't been sure about her suspicions but now she was. "But I'm not going to tell anyone about that...about you. That's your secret to keep. What I want you to do is help me find the barn I was held in. It was an old rickety barn. Not the beautiful barn at his house."

Martha's hand flew to her mouth as she gasped.

"I have to find that barn, Martha. I left proof in it. I

can prove I was in that building, but first I need to know where it is."

The door opened. Matthew walked in. His face turned red as he stared at Raven. "You have a lot of nerve showing up here, little lady. All those ugly accusations about Chuck. He's a good man. I can't believe I liked you. That I trusted you."

"He's not a good man, Sheriff. He's a monster. And I have to try to stop him. No, I will stop him." She turned back to Martha who was wiping away tears.

"Look what you've done. You've upset Martha. You need to leave. Now."

"I'm not the one who upset her, Sheriff. I came here to ask you to do your job. You told me that you wouldn't stop until you found the monster who kidnapped me and tried to kill me. Well, I remembered who did those things to me. Now it's time for you to keep your promise."

"I promised that when I thought you were honest. Not a liar."

"I'm not a liar, Sheriff. And you know that. You saw my broken body. You saw what he did to me."

"What someone did to you. Not Chuck. He's a good man. I'm not even sure if any of that even happened to you. You might have faked all of it. I'm closing my investigation. As of now."

"You know that's not true. You know I didn't make it up. You can't really believe I threw myself off a cliff. Or that I burnt myself like that. You saw the burn marks on my body. Nobody does that to themselves for any reason."

"Seems a little crazy to me, but there's all kind of crazy in this world. People love to be celebrities nowadays. I wouldn't put it past you that you did this whole thing so you could get famous."

"If that were true, why wouldn't I have used my name on the book?"

He stared at her. "Well…I'm not sure, but I know Chuck wouldn't have done the things you're saying."

"I have proof. I left proof in that barn. But I have to find the barn."

"What sort of proof?"

"I found a nail, and I scratched my name on the wooden windowsill. My name is in that barn. If you really think I made the whole thing up, then let's go find that barn. And either way, it will prove whether I'm lying or telling the truth."

He stared at her. He was thinking about it. She pushed on. "You said you've known Charles Whitman most of your life. Has he always lived in that fine house with that beautiful barn? Or is there another barn? A rickety, old wooden barn."

She saw the flicker of recognition in his eyes.

Would he tell the truth, or would he protect the monster?

52

Martha walked out from behind the counter and touched her husband's arm. "You'll never be able to forgive yourself, Matt, if you don't try to at least prove or disprove what she's saying."

"I don't need her to prove that Chuck's a good guy. We know that."

"He may not be the man you think he is," Her voice shook.

He turned toward his wife. "What are you saying, Martha?"

"I'm saying take her out to the old barn. Give her the chance to prove she's not lying."

He stared at the woman he loved. "If that's what you want."

"That's what I want."

"Let's go." He motioned at Raven and then as if just noticing Hunter asked, "Who are you?"

"I'm with her. I'm Deputy Hunter from the Holmes County Sheriff's Department in Ohio but in full disclosure I'm not here in an official capacity. I'm here as Raven's friend."

"Whatever. Let's go." He looked at Martha. "Are you coming with us?"

She shook her head. "Someone has to stay. It

might as well be me."

The sheriff walked toward the door but then went back to Martha. His arms went around her, and he whispered in her ear. She nodded and smiled. He turned and walked out with Hunter following behind.

Raven said, "I'll be right behind you. In a minute."

The two men walked out.

Raven turned back to Martha. "Are you OK?"

"I'm fine, dear. You go now. Go prove it for both of us." Her eyes filled with tears. "I'm sorry. I...I...really didn't know. I thought what he did to me was my fault. If I'd thought he was the one who hurt you, I would have...have stopped him."

"We'll stop him now. He's not hurting anyone else." She hugged her. "Thank you for your help. And don't worry, your secret is safe with me."

When she got to the car, Hunter was already in the back, so she got in the front.

Matthew glared at her. "What'd you say to Martha? Did you upset her even more?"

"I thanked her for believing in me."

"Yeah, I guess I wasn't too nice before. Sorry. This whole thing has been a shock to me. To all of us."

"So are you saying you believe me?"

"I know someone hurt you. I know you didn't make that up. I just think you're mistaken about who. That's all. But let's get out to that barn. Let's see what you can prove."

"Fair enough. So where are we going?"

"Chuck didn't grow up in the house where he lives now. He built that place about twenty years ago when he got married. The house he grew up in is long gone. It burned down, but the some of the outbuildings are still there. It was never sold after his parents died in it."

"They died in the fire?"

"Yep."

"What caused the fire?"

"Why? Are you going to accuse him of that too?"

"What other buildings?" Hunter asked from the back seat.

"Two barns and a silo."

"Maybe we should get a search warrant first." Hunter said from the backseat. "We don't want the evidence thrown out."

"Not necessary." The sheriff looked over at Raven. "He doesn't actually own it. His sister did but she donated it to the county a few months ago. It's going to become the Whitman Conservation Center and Park. At least that was the plan. Before."

That stopped the conversation.

His sister. Gracie had mentioned it after she did the title search. At the time, none of them thought it was significant. Apparently, they were wrong.

The sheriff turned onto Route 9, the same road Whitman's current house was on. A few minutes later he made a right turn, and they bumped down a long lane. Her gaze took in the area. Nothing looked familiar. But that wasn't too surprising. She'd never seen anything outside of the room that was her prison. Wherever the house had been, it wasn't there now. Only a field and grass.

The sheriff pulled up to the larger barn. "Here we go. So where's this proof you claim is here?"

"I don't know which building I was in. But I'll know when I see inside them. I scratched my name on a wooden windowsill and the date. The last one I remembered anyway."

Hunter took hold of her hand.

She wondered if he noticed that she was shaking. He squeezed her hand as they walked inside the larger of the two barns. They walked from one end to the other. She peered inside the smaller rooms. "This isn't the place."

"Yeah, that's what I figured." The sheriff said. "I know Chuck isn't capable of the things you're accusing him of."

They left the larger barn and headed toward the smaller building.

A motor broke the silence.

"What's that?" Hunter asked.

Sounded like a golf cart.

Raven's world turned wavy. She'd been in a golf cart the night he'd tried to kill her, but God had protected her then, and He would protect her now. She took a deep breath and the world came back in focus.

Charles Whitman pulled up in front of the barn, blocking their way. He stepped out of the golf cart. "What are you doing here, Matt? And with her? You need to arrest her."

"She claims there's proof here that you kidnapped her, Chuck."

"That's ridiculous and you know it. Besides, this is private property. You have no right to be here. You need to leave, Sheriff. And you need to do your job and take her in custody. I'll call my security detail to come for her." He pulled out a phone.

"I'll arrest her after I check out her claims."

Charles Whitman stepped in front of them, blocking them from the entrance. "This is private property. Please leave."

"I'm not doing that. And you don't own this

property. Your sister donated it to the county a few months ago, so I have a right to go in without your permission. She wanted it to be a surprise for you. A park named after you."

Charles Whitman's eyes bulged.

"Now step out of the way."

He didn't move, so they walked around him. The moment she walked inside, her world turned wavy and a wave of nausea hit her. She grabbed Hunter's arm. "This is the place."

"Are you sure?"

"Yeah, we had a fight over here. I tried to hit him with the rake, but he grabbed it from me and started hitting me with it. I passed out and when I woke up, I was in a golf cart. He drove me somewhere and threw me off the cliff." She stopped walking and pointed in the small room. "There. That's the room. That's where he chained me up. Like a dog."

"So where's this supposed proof?" Matthew Borden didn't sound nearly as confident as he had at the station.

"In there. Look at the window. You'll see my name scratched in the wood on the sill."

The sheriff walked over.

Hunter did the same, pulling out his camera as he did. He started snapping pictures without saying a word.

Matthew looked at her. "It's there. Your name and the date. I can't believe this. It's true. All of it."

"You did it, Raven. You proved he's your monster." Hunter said. "I'm so proud of you."

Charles Whitman charged into the room and stared at the windowsill. "It's a lie. All of it's a lie. She sneaked down here earlier and put her name there.

She's crazy."

"Sorry, Chuck." The sheriff walked toward him. "You have the right to remain silent. Anything you say can and will be used against you in a court of law. You have the right to an attorney. If you cannot afford an attorney, one will be provided for you. Do you understand the rights I have just read to you? With these rights in mind, do you wish to speak to me?"

"It's a lie. It's a lie. I'm going to be the next President of the United States. You can't do this to me."

The sheriff looked at Raven. "I'll call the State Crime lab. You said your DNA will be on this."

"I spit on it. And not just there. On every wall. I put spit all over the place. I knew I was going to die. I wanted to leave proof that I was here. Proof that he was a monster."

The sheriff pulled out his phone.

"You can't believe this woman. She's just a vindictive, celebrity-seeking narcissist, Matt. You know how reporters are."

"I've told you your rights. Now put your hands behind your back, Chuck. Please don't make this harder than it has to be."

"Don't you talk to me about my rights. I'm Senator Charles Whitman. I'm going to be the next President of the United States. You can't arrest me. You have no right. Get off my land." He ran out of the room.

The sheriff chased after him.

Whitman picked up a red gas can. "You've got no proof." He started splashing gas around the building.

"Stop it, Chuck. It's over."

"It's not over. I'll pay you a lot of money. We'll get rid of them, and no one has to ever know they were even here."

"I'd know." Matthew Borden pulled out the handcuffs from his belt. "Now put your hands behind your back."

Charles Whitman pulled out a lighter.

Matthew lunged at him, but it was too late.

Whitman dropped the lit lighter on the floor where he'd poured gasoline only moments before. The blaze whooshed as the fire met the gasoline.

"Call 911." Matthew yelled at no one in particular.

Raven looked at Hunter. He was already calling. She looked around. There. A water spigot. Rushing to it, she turned on the water and grabbed the hose. In the few seconds it took to get back to the fire, she couldn't believe how it had grown. She started spraying.

"Here give it to me," Matthew yelled.

"No. You help get him in handcuffs." The fire was spreading. This couldn't happen. She wouldn't let this place burn down. It was her proof. She kept spraying as Hunter ran to help the sheriff. As Matt attempted to put Charles in cuffs, a fight ensued.

She kept spraying.

Hunter pulled Whitman off the Sheriff. With both of them working together, they got the cuffs on him.

Fire truck sirens sounded in the distance.

But it was OK. The fire was out, though still smoldering. It hadn't gone into her room. The evidence was safe.

"I started recording on my phone and now have evidence he tried to bribe Matt, too." Hunter took the hose out of her hand and brought her into the circle of his arms. "It's over, sweetheart. It's over."

53

"Oh, my. Oh, my." Lydia looked over at Raven. "I can't believe all you went through. You poor thing. No wonder you're afraid of the dark."

"That bone fragment from your leg that the forensic team found in the barn was the clincher," Hunter said. "Before that, everything could be discounted because your car's license plate was seen on Whitman's security cameras when you went to his house that day you went to look. There were a few people who thought you might have planted evidence then."

"She would never do that!" Amanda was indignant.

"I know that," Hunter's arm tightened around Raven's shoulders. "But others didn't. When they found that bone and did the forensics on it, that's when the police finally believed her. It was impossible for her to have planted it. Plus, she was already healed by the time anyone saw her near the place. And she wasn't in any shape to plant evidence before that. My phone recording of Whitman trying to bribe Matt at the barn also helped."

They were in Raven's living room. Gracie, Amanda, and Todd. And of course, Hunter.

They'd watched the special on Charles Whitman, III's crimes and his arrest together, and were now watching the primary results.

"I was afraid of the dark, Lydia, but I think that will be a thing of the past." Raven addressed her friend's concern. "The night of my party, I was sitting in my closet. I was so afraid. Of everything. But when I turned to some verses in the Bible, peace came over me. It's been better since then."

"A peace that defies human understanding." Gracie said. "I know I have that peace too. It makes no sense, but God is God. And He keeps His promises."

"Amen," Hunter said.

"I'm surprised, you're not in New York at some fancy TV station," Amanda said. "Now that you're so famous. The woman who survived."

"They asked me to, but I really don't want that kind of life. I want the life I have here in Charm, Ohio. This is exactly where I want to be."

"What about our bakery?" Lydia asked.

"We're opening that bakery, and you're going to teach me how to make these delicious cookies and cakes. Not to mention that chocolate cream pie." Raven picked up another cookie. "But for the next few weeks, I'll be busy writing my new book. Once it's done, I'll be ready to bake these amazing cookies."

"Yeah, I'll believe that when I see it, sis."

"Me, too." Todd chimed in. "I've had your cooking."

"I don't know. Her lasagna was pretty good. Better than good."

"Thank you, Hunter. I'm glad someone appreciates my cooking." It felt so good to sit here and to feel truly safe. Now that Charles Whitman was behind bars, he couldn't hurt her or anyone else.

"What's going on with the investigation?" Amanda asked.

"Oh, they're finding out all sorts of interesting things. He did withdraw a hundred thousand dollars from one of his accounts in cash. It fits the timeline for when Sydney deposited it in her account. Other women have come forward as well."

"He really is a monster." Amanda shuddered. "Can you imagine what might have happened if he was elected?"

Hunter squeezed Raven's hand. "God saved you for a purpose. In spite of how afraid you were, you listened to God. We should all learn to be more like you."

She grinned. "Oh, stop it. You're embarrassing me. After all, I'm just a narcissistic celebrity-seeking reporter."

"Speaking of reporters, I hear Shanley's in trouble with the network. And that her cameraman's been promoted to an on-camera personality."

"He certainly deserves it," Hunter said. "If he hadn't had the courage to put that video on the air, all of this might not have happened."

"Yes, he does."

After everyone left, Hunter stayed behind to help clean up. He carried dishes to her while she washed them. Then he grabbed a towel and began drying them. Looking up from the soapy dishwater, she said, "I need to put a dishwasher in here."

"I can do that for you if you want. But I thought you might be moving to New York or Washington. I'm sure you can write your ticket now if you want to be a reporter. And a TV reporter at that."

"I already said I'm right where I want to be. I'm going to bake cookies and try my hand at writing a novel."

"Are you sure this is where you want to be?"

"Not only am I where I want to be, but I'm with the man I want to be with." She dried her hands on the towel. "I know you told me that I wasn't ready for a relationship but..."

He smiled and moved closer. "I might have been mistaken about that." His arms went around her.

"I'm pretty sure you were wrong."

She leaned closer and closer...until their lips met.

Author's Note

Dear Readers,

Secrets can be a good thing. A surprise birthday party. Christmas time secrets. A secret proposal that took lots of planning and secrets to get you to the right place at the right time. But there are other secrets. Secrets that hurt. Secrets that hinder. Secrets that destroy. Secrets that make you hide from people and God. I know all about those kind of secrets.

For many years, I lived a secret life not of my own making, but still it was my choice. Because of my choices, I ran from God. The more I ran the more miserable I became. It was only when I stopped living with the secrets that I found my way back to God.

God was right there waiting for me and since then God's helped me rebuild my life. A life filled with love, peace, and joy—in spite of having brain tumors (non-cancerous, but not benign).

When you keep secrets because you're afraid of what other people will think, then they aren't the right kind of secrets. Like Raven, it's not always easy to share secrets but as Raven learned, bringing the secrets to light will take you out of the darkness.

And God will be there waiting for you with open arms.

God Bless & Good Reading.

Thank you...

for purchasing this Harbourlight title. For other inspirational stories, please visit our on-line bookstore at www.pelicanbookgroup.com.

For questions or more information, contact us at customer@pelicanbookgroup.com.

Harbourlight Books
The Beacon in Christian Fiction™
an imprint of Pelican Book Group
www.pelicanbookgroup.com

Connect with Us
www.facebook.com/Pelicanbookgroup
www.twitter.com/pelicanbookgrp

To receive news and specials, subscribe to our bulletin
http://pelink.us/bulletin

May God's glory shine through
this inspirational work of fiction.

AMDG

You Can Help!

At Pelican Book Group it is our mission to entertain readers with fiction that uplifts the Gospel. It is our privilege to spend time with you awhile as you read our stories.

We believe you can help us to bring Christ into the lives of people across the globe. And you don't have to open your wallet or even leave your house!

Here are 3 simple things you can do to help us bring illuminating fiction™ to people everywhere.

1) If you enjoyed this book, write a positive review. Post it at online retailers and websites where readers gather. And share your review with us at reviews@pelicanbookgroup.com (this does give us permission to reprint your review in whole or in part.)

2) If you enjoyed this book, recommend it to a friend in person, at a book club or on social media.

3) If you have suggestions on how we can improve or expand our selection, let us know. We value your opinion. Use the contact form on our web site or e-mail us at customer@pelicanbookgroup.com

God Can Help!

Are you in need? The Almighty can do great things for you. Holy is His Name! He has mercy in every generation. He can lift up the lowly and accomplish all things. Reach out today.

Do not fear: I am with you; do not be anxious: I am your God. I will strengthen you, I will help you, I will uphold you with my victorious right hand.

~Isaiah 41:10 (NAB)

We pray daily, and we especially pray for everyone connected to Pelican Book Group—that includes you! If you have a specific need, we welcome the opportunity to pray for you. Share your needs or praise reports at http://pelink.us/pray4us